◆ ◆ ◆

Like Ripples in Water

◆ ◆ ◆

Like Ripples in Water

A Collection in Two Parts

Garrett Willis

© 2017 Garrett Willis
All rights reserved.

ISBN-13: 9781979629591
ISBN-10: 1979629595
Library of Congress Control Number: 2017917573
CreateSpace Independent Publishing Platform
North Charleston, South Carolina

As a whole, this book is dedicated to my mom.
Because you created me, I am able to create these words,
but these words still fail to describe how much you mean to me.

Part I

A collection of eight interconnected short stories

Dedicated to Weston. Thank you for the endless cups of coffee, and thank you for your endless friendship.
You deserve so much more than I have to offer.

Loneliness

A nd so he lived his first seventeen years in a blur: nothing new, everything old, and with no one at all. Along the lines of his academics, looks, and social skills, he was completely average—if not slightly below in one or two of those categories. He only talked a few times a day, and mainly only when being spoken to. He was fine being in his head; he was fine being with himself, being alone. He dreamed, both while awake and asleep, of being the hero. Saving the day, saving the world, saving the girl. He didn't know what girl. Just a girl who would ultimately fall in love with him due to his heroic actions.

A year of this stagnation passed, but he never grew tired of his fantasies. He was eighteen now, two months away from wearing a robe, and he couldn't care less. All his care was allocated to that girl. People often remark that it isn't healthy to obsess over some- one or something that doesn't exist, but he had nothing real worth obsessing over. He drew this imaginary girl in his journal (the same journal his mom would eventually discover and cry), and he would fall asleep with the image of her hair, being swept up by the wind, grazing over his face.

And then he saw her. He was in a queer spot on the street in Santa Monica. Was he from Santa Monica? No. Some family mem- bers were, and he was paying them a visit. But he saw her across the street, in-between the passing cars, by the pier. He rubbed his eyes for a second, making sure it wasn't some beautiful dust par- ticle in his eye. And then he looked back in her direction and she looked in his, and he saw nothing but her and she saw everything but him, and he knew it and she knew nothing. His heart sank, and his knees quivered. The weight her existence put on him from across the street was something meant for someone better than he. He watched her put a hand through her brown hair. He couldn't help but notice how the sun reflected off her strands, and how it made her seem as if she glowed. As if she were angelic.

It's all cheesy and romantic hogwash, but that's how this poor little sheltered boy was. Because of this girl, in a burgundy skirt, he seemingly forgot how to breathe. He took so long to inhale that the air particles around him grew concerned. After a few moments of oxygen deprivation, he inhaled through his nostrils, and watched her turn away.

"No," he whispered. He rushed to the stoplight, too nervous to be thankful that he could immediately use the crosswalk. What was he going to do? Go be a creep and tap her on the shoulders and confess his love to some strange girl who might not even know English? Who might have a boyfriend? Who might not be into men? His social skills lacked luster, but in this moment, above all else, he lacked intelligence. As he approached her slightly bare back, he put up a hand to tap her, but he quickly realized he wouldn't be able to produce the necessary sounds needed to form what are called "words." So he put his hand down, and relegated himself to following her around like an utter creep. A minute or two in, or an eternity to him, she pulled out her phone from her purse that, with a strap, lay on her left shoulder. He could see the phone's screen was lit up in her hand. She answered it.

"Hi Amy. No, it's fine; what's going on?" she said into the phone.

"Oh my God." He was baffled. Not that he could say words, but that her voice was something out of heaven. He put his hands on his cheeks with his mouth opened wide, and slowly dragged his hands down. He was in shock, for some reason, and the passersby probably thought there was something wrong with his head. She continued talking, and while looking at her perfectly symmetrical shoulder blades, he decided that this was fate and this moment was given to him by the universe and he has to have her and that, for once, he was special.

He followed her, but as his daydreaming overtook him, he imagined all the things lonely guys imagine: how he would hold her, how he would kiss her, how he would make her a great meal because he read somewhere that women love men who can cook. God he was lonely. And yes, of course he imagined the more sexual things, as everyone who is older than thirteen has, but he wanted more than sexual intimacy. He just wanted to be close. He was tired of being distant from others, of being away from others, of being unnecessarily alone. He wanted a friend. He wanted a lover. He wanted to be loved. And so he decided that he needed her.

He wasn't going to do anything unspeakable or *bad*. He wasn't that kind of person, or that kind of sheltered. He came to the conclusion that he would win her just as he had won all the other girls in his dreams: he would save her.

So he followed her and watched her legs striate as the force of the ground came upon them. He watched her skirt sway in the dusky breeze, and the world seemed all right and all terrible at the same time. All right in the sense that he was close, so close, and that life with her could actually begin in any moment. But terrible in the sense that they were still a lifetime apart; he knew nothing about her, only that she existed, and she knew nothing about him, not even his existence. Her phone was away now, and she continued on down the road, bewildering him as to where she was headed. He decided he would follow her to the ends of the world, as cliche and incorrect as that sounds. He walked and watched, walked and watched, walked and dreamed. He didn't have a damn clue as to what he was getting himself into, but he knew that she would be worth it. He never considered if she would have thought he would be worth it. She stopped at a little food stand to get something to drink and he decided a smoothie sounded good, too.

As they were waiting in line, him behind her, she put her hand into her sea of hair. He saw, boy did he see this, and the butterflies rose to his mouth. For a moment he believed he would vomit, but he ended up not completely ruining his chance with this stranger. She got a strawberry smoothie and so, obviously, he did too. As they waited on the other end of the stand for their drinks, he actually stood beside her. She even glanced at him. His peripheral was burning and his heart was smoldering.

She saw me, he repeated, in his head, a thousand times in a minute. One of the men in the stand called out a strawberry smoothie, and this socially-inept person had the audacity to believe that his smoothie would be made before hers. He accidentally cut her off, without his even noticing, and grabbed the smoothie.

"Um, excuse me," she said to him. He choked on his own existence, still not acknowledging what he had just done. It took him a moment. But he eventually looked at her.

"Yes, what is it?" Smooth. He did, however, notice the mistake in his word choice and tone. He was still holding her smoothie.

"I believe that smoothie is mine. I ordered before you. Did you order a strawberry one as well?"

His face became engulfed in metaphorical flame, and he stared down at the drink in question. *Shit.*

"Excuse me?" she asked again.

Shit! Say something you idiot! He looked back up at her. She had a worried smile, with a hint of annoyance in her furrowed brow. "Oh, ha ha, sorry. Here."

He stretched out his hand, clearly showing the shaking of the smoothie. She reached up for the drink, and placed her hand toward the top of the container. As she applied pressure to the container, and began pulling it toward herself, he felt her pinky graze his index finger. And then he knew he had fallen in love. He felt this in his heart—or his soul or brain, wherever scientists claim love exists. He didn't care about the logistics; he cared about the sensation. This is why he was still alive: for her. At least, that's what, in that moment, he believed. This was the universe's ultimate plan for him: to give a smoothie to a girl, have her atoms repel his, and then call it love.

"Sorry about that," he finally said, after staring at her like a ghoul for too long.

She smiled. "Don't worry about it. I believe they called your drink." He turned around, looked at the small counter at the edge of the stand and saw his smoothie. He was well aware of the symbols behind cherries, so he had ordered two on top of his smoothie. He walked, trying his best to seem carefree, and grabbed his drink. The man was staring from the blender in the stand, so he thanked the man and decided to put a dollar in the tip jar. He turned around.

And then she was gone.

His eyes widened, he rushed, frantically, onto the sidewalk. Throwing his head side to side, he felt his eyes burning. His heart raced and the tears boiled to the edge of his eyes. He couldn't decide whether to go left or right; he was unsure of it all. Of everything. He was so close, so why would the universe betray him so quickly? Why bait him, hook him, and then pull him up to another planet lightyears away from the girl in the skirt? Time stood still and wrapped around him all at once. The cars passed, and he grew sick from all his spinning trying to find her. It was moot. He had searched up and down the sidewalk they had walked, and even went into nearby buildings, but it was moot. She was gone. And then the sun disappeared, too.

He couldn't sleep that night because of the angel he had let go and the bed in his family's spare bedroom was hard and he was sick to his stomach and he just wanted to vanish. It's always sad to lose someone, but he had never necessarily experienced this. But to contradict that, he had never actually experienced her. He had a fantasized version of this person he saw from across the street, not the real her. But either way, he told himself, reiterating it through every fiber in his body over and over, that he was heartbroken. He told himself that the universe had a sick sense of humor, and that no benevolence could be found in the cosmos, only fire and darkness and loneliness.

So he lay in bed all night, and he might have fallen asleep for thirty minutes here and there, but he was woken up every time his damn mind went back to her walking in front of him. The next night was the same. After spending all day on the streets looking for this ghost, he went back to the house and lay in bed, looking up at the ceiling, wishing to sink into the mattress and fade out of being. The next day and night were the same. And then he went home. And life, as it always has, continued. He went back to school. A month went by. He was a month away from graduating.

Things were winding down in school, as the teachers were essentially wrapping up their curriculums. He had passed his classes, even though he had slumped quite a bit in the past month. Good thing almost no assignments were due, but he didn't care. Life turned gray to him, and he lost interest in tomorrow. The universe had tricked him once before, and he would not let it get his hopes up ever again. Never would he allow the universe to play its sick games on him; he was not some pawn for the universe to expend at its own satisfaction. This high school senior was always a little melodramatic in his own mind, but he had gone overboard with this whole Santa Monica fiasco. But he didn't think so. He saw his moment of greatness flicker right beside him next to the smoothie stand. And then the flicker died. Very melodramatic indeed.

He was sitting in English class, as he had every Monday, Tuesday, Wednesday, Thursday, and Friday, and the teacher got a phone call. She walked back over to her desk and picked up the phone.

"Room forty-four," she said into the phone receiver. A moment passed: "Ok… Yeah, that's fine… No, she can come now… All right… All right, bye. Bye." The teacher hung up the phone and then walked back to the center of the front of the room. She looked at the students with her characteristic look that says, *Shut the hell up; I have something to say.* The class slowly quieted.

"A new student is on her way," she began, "and I don't want anyone screwing around. Please be courteous and welcoming to her." She remained silent for a moment, and the awkward silence began to accumulate in-between the bodies of the thirty-odd students. As the teacher opened her mouth to say something else, the door knob made a noise.

And then she walked through the door.

He was hardly paying attention throughout all of class, let alone when the teacher began talking about the new student or when the universe had seemingly asked for forgiveness. He was staring out the window to his left when she walked through the door, and it wasn't until he heard a slight breath from a few of the students did he decide to turn his neck toward the front of the room. And there she was, and there he was, existing in the same room together, breathing the same air. The sun was far too universal; everyone gets sunlight from that—but this, he never imagined he would be able to breathe the same air as her again. He hadn't even dreamed about it; perhaps his subconscious had, but not him, not actively. He thoughtlessly gripped the edges of his desk and his brain stem erupted: his heart became a rocket, ready to pioneer him to Neptune, and his breathing became shallow and quick. He was hyperventilating at the speed of love, and he was not about to slow down.

He stared at her fervently, afraid that at any moment she might disappear just as before. Instead, he watched her smile to the students in their desks, and then slowly take a seat near him. He was too stunned to wish for her to sit next to him, so he ended up having to stare at her from his right peripheral, a few rows across. The teacher went on with the lesson, and as the event finally recorded itself in his mind, he found himself growing paranoid. He was paranoid of all the other guys in the room. Paranoid that they might try to talk to her. That they might want her. That she might want one of them. He knew he would have to act quickly. After class he would be the first to talk to her. There was no way in hell he would let Ron, who was sitting in front of her, talk to her first. *Screw Ron.*

As his eyes shot between the hands of the clock and the side image of her figure, he found himself sweating profusely. He couldn't help it; his body was running in fight or flight mode. He somewhat believed that this moment, depending on his choices, would truly decide his fate. So of course he was nervous, and of course he was excited. He had fallen into a black pit, and with one glance of her again, he was instantly swept back to the surface by a whirlwind of hope. It's weird how love can do this to someone, or, at least, do this to a hormonal eighteen-year-old who had barely even talked to girls before. He was inexperienced in this subject, but he figured love wasn't a job; it didn't require experience. Love, to him, was a staple of life, and the only requirement to obtain it was simply to be alive. His thought processes are completely watered-down and simplistic: love is a job. It takes work. It requires time, affection, understanding, desire, and a multi-faceted connection to someone else. It's a full-time job, and being fired from love can be disastrous. But sometimes people aren't fired from love; sometimes they just quit.

The bell rang and he threw his school copy of *The Aeneid* into his backpack and haphazardly crossed in front of the rows until he found himself at the head of her row. He tried to play it cool. He tried so hard. But he watched her graciously put away her things and he couldn't help but find that he had no idea where to put his hands. He fiddled with them, and he tried every place imaginable, but they all seemed out-of-place and noticeable. As she put her bag around her shoulder, he ended with his right hand on that side's strap of his backpack, and the other hand in the left pocket. She looked forward and saw him standing there. Her eyes lit up for a second, as her eyebrows raised, and he hoped she had remembered him.

He stood there. She sat there. After a few moments of trying his hardest to keep eye contact, he could no longer bare the sensation and he looked away. She slowly stood up, all while keeping her gaze toward the awkward boy standing six feet in front of her. She began walking toward him, or at least toward the front of the classroom, and he looked back at her. She was smiling.

As she approached him she said, "Weren't you the one who took my smoothie?"

He was elated. She had remembered him. He wasn't invisible to her at the time; he was memorable. "Yeah, that was me. Sorry about that again," he said, nervously.

She laughed, "Don't worry about it. It's so weird that you go here. I just transferred from Santa Monica High School."

"Very cool," he said, not wanting her to leave the classroom. "If you want, I can show you around the school. It's lunch time for our grade." He suddenly felt a surge of confidence and adrenaline. In an instant his mind was clear and he was certain, for once, about what he needed to do in his life, in that moment.

"Oh, that would be perfect!"

He showed her around the school, talked to her about the town, and he learned her name and she learned his. He continued to see nothing but her and she began to see him. They had the next class together, and he was able to get her to sit in the empty seat in front of him. They did not have the same class after that, but he was able to choke up the words to ask her to meet him after school, and she agreed.

They spent all afternoon together, and he grew more and more in love with this person he was just barely getting to know. He didn't dare ruin any moment by bringing up any asinine questions such as, *Do you think you could love me? Will you, oh stranger, be my girlfriend?* He really wanted things to go naturally, and they did exactly that. Everything flowed smoothly, just as her hair did in the sunset. He knew time was running out thanks to the sunlight retreating. He knew he would lie awake all night in bed, waiting for the sun to make its round and come back to fight another day. So, with a few minutes of light left in his reinvigorated life, they hugged in a park, and he lingered, and then she turned and began walking. She insisted on her going home alone, so he left it at that. He decided to watch her stride before he would turn and go home. As soon as she was out of his sight, he took a deep breath and relaxed his arms and allowed tears to collect in his lower eyelids.

And then the bell rang.

He found himself sitting in his English class, tears lightly rolling down his cheeks. He had been daydreaming. He looked to his right only to find no girl sitting to his right. The students were hurriedly leaving the classroom, unaware of what had just happened in this boy's mind. *It was so vivid, so real*, he thought. Instead of getting up, he put his head down and began to weep. The teacher heard his muffled anguish, and slowly crossed over to him from her desk.

"What's the matter?" the teacher asked.

He took a moment, but eventually he lifted up his head and wiped away his tears, his eyes remaining bloodshot. He stared ahead. The weight of his life became unbearably heavy. The pressure of his life engulfed him, and then he felt the Big Crunch. He simply shrugged his shoulders: "Nothing."

He got up, packed his bag, thoughtlessly put his hands in his pocket, and walked out to the front of the school. As a senior he was allowed to go off campus for lunch, and so he did just that. He walked down the sidewalk which would eventually connect, through adjacent paths and trails, to his front door. He walked for thirty minutes, keeping his head down the whole time. He kicked every rock in his path, and cursed each one he missed. He got to his front door and slid his key into the deadbolt, taking a second to breathe in the outside air. He walked into his house, pushed his excited dog aside, and ascended the stairs to his bedroom. Once he got into his room he chucked his backpack into the corner, knowing he wouldn't have any use for it again.

Lying on his bed for more than fifteen minutes, he noticed he couldn't bring himself to cry. There was no point. He reached under his mattress and pulled out his worn journal. This journal had been with him through it all. This journal, although heavily used for drawings of imaginary girls, was his autobiography. It was a testament to his failures and his dreams. But mainly his failures, he often believed.

He flipped through some of his more recent passages, and once he got to the first blank page, he pulled out a pen from his pocket and wrote a few words. After a moment of gazing at the words, he put the pen in the journal and closed it as much as it would. He got up, walked out of his room, went downstairs, and allowed the quiet of his house to envelope him. This silence spoke to him, telling him this was his life now. No one in it, and nothing to stir up a commotion, or even to disrupt the silence. But he would not have that. He walked into his garage and found a thick chunk of manila rope. He went back upstairs.

In a blur, but with concise and smooth motions, he tied the rope into a noose and draped it over the railing that overlooked the downstairs. He grabbed his journal and put it down by the railing. He tied a knot with the rope around the railing in order to secure its place. He then placed the noose around his neck. In the few moments before he jumped, he didn't think about his family, or if he were being selfish, or even of love. He thought only of loss and recovery. He lost the girl and lost the love, but he will regain freedom. No longer will he be tied to the emotions and disappointments of life. And perhaps he would be able to dream about her again. He took a breath.

And then he jumped.

He killed himself at 1:12PM, but his mom did not discover him until 5:27PM. She walked through the door and saw him dangling five feet off the ground. She dropped her bags and called her husband, and then the cops. She didn't know what to do, so she went and waited outside until they all arrived. As the coroners got him down, she was able to push her way up the stairs. Next to the railing, before being forced back downstairs, she saw his journal. She quickly grabbed it.

Once she got back outside, she immediately opened the journal to where the pen was stuck in the seam. She read the last passage which he wrote:

The universe has left me. So I am leaving the universe.

And then she cried.

Failure

December 14th

Sometimes I think of myself as a person of the seasons. What I mean by this is that who I am sometimes wholly depends on the season. For instance, every winter my emotions tend to swing in the cold breeze. I am still who I am, as I always have been, but I am more prone to certain emotional leanings or awkward thought processes. Awkward in the sense that I would not normally think of such things. But spring is a good time, for the most part. I spend most days happy and relaxed. It's a good time of year. Summer is *okay*; it's a little too hot for me, but I've just never enjoyed outside labor, or picnics when it is 108 degrees out. I mean, what the hell? Why?

Now, don't get me wrong; I'm a man, okay? I'm not a very emotional person—at least not physically that is. I'll admit that I tend to keep things bottled up and whatnot. But it is true that I have only cried three times in my adult life: once when my son was born, once when my son died, and, more recently, when my ex-wife decided to leave me for another man. Which was very recent. Like, three weeks ago recent. So there's that.

Veronica, her name is. She's a very nice lady, or at least she was. It would be a lie for me to say I don't have any current resentments toward her. Because, in all honesty, ~~she ripped out my heart, and I think my soul went with it, as it nested in one of the chambers~~. Sorry, that sounds pretty stupid. Maybe I'll cross that out. Anyhow, she and I were married for twenty-four years; we got married when I was twenty and she was nineteen. Things were simpler back then. But things happen that happen to every life, and it got complicated.

Life is complicated, I suppose; I mean, it took life at least a billion years after the formation of the earth to pop up. And now here we are, 3.5 billion years later. 3.5 billion years of atoms doing random, ridiculous stuff, and here I am, emotionally distraught over a piece of life that occupied twenty-four years of my existence. Why did things evolve to this? I don't understand why life would want all these emotions to get in the way of survival. Or perhaps there's something more, something greater, something grand, and I've missed it all this time.

But I digress. My therapist, upon assessing my current situation and state-of-mind, has asked me to start a journal, and told me to write how I *feel* in this journal. I should not be writing about evolution and stuff. But I'm not good with this emotional stuff. I never was. I don't think I ever will be.

I think I'll write about Veronica—how we were, how life was, and whatever else comes to mind. However, I'm going to keep this short; I don't like this crap.

Marriage is like life, I believe. Just like life, it has its ups and its downs. One moment you feel like swinging your partner around while listening to Frank Sinatra. But other times you just want to be alone, undisturbed. Sometimes I would long, even after fifteen years of marriage, to kiss her lips and hold her head, my fingers combing through the back of her hair. And other times I would want nothing more than to tell her to shut up, that her lips move too much, that they produce too much noise. But I never did say that.

But now, in retrospect, I don't blame her; it's just marriage. It's just that closeness with another human being. You long to occupy the same space, but then you find yourself suffocating with nowhere to go. I love her still, even though her love has been redirected to another man. Or maybe he stole that love. Maybe it still rightfully belongs to me. I'm not sure if I ever did anything to take away that privilege of receiving Veronica's love. Or perhaps he did something greater than I ever could for her. I don't know if I will ever know.

Anyways, I feel slightly lost. It's almost as if I'm in a forest, but my trail is nearby. I *know* it's there, but I'm just not quite sure exactly where it is. I've wandered off it for a little too long, and I've gone a little too far. Finding it shouldn't impossible—I don't think. It'll just take some time. And now, with my once-family now completely gone, I've got nothing but unoccupied space and unallocated time.

I also feel hurt. Or maybe betrayed. Maybe it's a mixture of the two. Either way, Veronica really screwed me over. Since I got the boot I've only dreamt about the memories we had. It really sucks, to be honest. I've got all this footage in my head, but no one wants to ever see it—not even me. But what am I to do with it? *Nothing* would be the best option, I suppose, but instead I'm stuck with chemicals reacting in my brain in a certain way that make my neurons fire up the old reel. And then she pops up and I enter REM sleep. ~~God is she lovely in my memories~~.

One memory I've dreamt about three times now is this one instance where Veronica and I and our son, when he was only six, went to the fair:

It was a town fair, so there was only about three rides, but I remember we went on one of the rides that's kind of like a box, and it all spins. The three of us went into our own little cubby and I sat on the opposite side of her. I remember looking into her eyes, in the the dimly lit cubby, and I allowed life—reality—to melt away. It was only she and I there. She gave me a funny look and then she smiled that smile that always looked like the crescent moon, and so I gave her my own crooked smile. The ride began spinning, and her hair got caught up with the wind and momentum the ride was creating. I could tell she was slightly frightened, but it made my heart speed up seeing her shocked face, and her wavy hair dancing around. She locked eyes with me once again, and mouthed "I hate you," jokingly. Her hair consumed the free space around her, and even spilled over to our son sitting next to her. I could tell he was annoyed, but it only made me enjoy their company even more. And, as always, the fantasy aspect of the dream would take over, and her hair would begin growing infinitely, filling up the entire cubby, drowning my son and me.

Each time I've dreamt this I have woken up with a racing, aching heart, and a sweat-drenched bed in an empty room

I don't quite know why my dreams take me back to times like these. Maybe I loved my ~~wife~~ ex-wife more back then. Or differently. She was definitely different back then, but I guess I was as well. I remember when we first started dating. She being left-handed, and my being right-handed, it was always kind of awkward for us at movie theaters: she would sit on the left side of me, so we would hold each other with our non-dominant hands. It wasn't until we were married did I propose she sit on my right so that we could hold each other with our best hands. I also thought it would be nice to feel her wedding ring in my hand. She agreed. And it was nice.

It took awhile, but the awkwardness of our new seating arrangement eventually subsided, and it began feeling much more comfortable. But the problem, now, with her new boyfriend, is wondering where she sits. Does she sit on his right side now?

I don't know; I think things would be different—for the better—if my son were still alive. He would be graduating in the spring of this school year. I remember he had been accepted to Cal State Long Beach. He was so close to graduating high school. But stuff happens. Life happens. And then life ends. Sometimes at one's own control, I suppose.

But yes, if my son were still alive, I think Veronica and I would still be together. There wouldn't have been that tortuous distance that crept in between us, or the crushing silence that snuck up on us. If my son were still here, I think Veronica would still be sitting on my right side at the theater. But that's a reality I'm no longer living in, I guess.

Connections

my lets out an exasperated sigh, puts her head into her folded arms, and moans something unintelligible.

Grace, who is sitting on the opposite side of the dorm room on her bed, looks up from her laptop. "What did you say?"

Amy slowly puts her head up as Grace watches. "I said I'm already over this whole college thing."

"What?" Grace laughs. "We're barely a month in."

"I know. And I'm already over it. I have so much homework and crap to do."

"Well, so do I. But I actually stay in to study. You always go out to 'experience college life,' as you say."

"Shut up. I'm going to buckle down," Amy says. There's a moment of silence, and then Amy thumps her head back into her arms. "Starting tomorrow."

Grace puts her laptop on her bed and begins to stand up. She is wearing jeans and a teal shirt with the words "Carpe Sleepem" printed in black. Even in the dim light of the dorm room her hazel eyes still capture and reflect an absurd amount of light.

She stands by the side of her bed for a moment, then shuts her eyes and stretches. Her slender arms, sprinkled with a few freckles, stretch as if to touch the ceiling. After a much-needed yawn, she wipes the baby tears from the corner of her almond eyes. She looks at Amy, who still has her head down.

"I'm going to go get dinner," Grace says.

Amy immediately perks her head up. "I'm coming too!"

Grace walks over to her closet and pulls out a dark blue sweater. Amy follows suit by pulling her jacket off her desk chair. Her jacket is salmon colored, which is her favorite color.

"All right, let's go," Grace says.

"Oh, hold on," Amy replies, looking around the room. "I can't remember where I put my phone." She searches for a minute or two and finally finds it under her backpack, where she placed both on her bed hours ago. Amy nods at Grace, and they leave.

As they walk down the hall of their residence building, Amy finds herself caught up in the hours of social media updates she missed out on due to studying. Grace notices this, laughs, and makes a conscious decision to leave her phone in her pocket. Grace feels that Amy is sometimes too concerned with the world in her electronic device, but unbeknownst to Grace, Amy often thinks that Grace must have self-esteem issues deep down since she doesn't have social media accounts. The truth is, Grace is perfectly fine with who she is, and, for most of her life, has been.

Grace and Amy have known each other since they were children. Amy's parents moved to California when she was only seven, and since she is eighteen now, she has known Grace longer than she hasn't. Grace wasn't the first, second, or even third person to talk to Amy; those prizes are awarded to boys who were ballsy enough at that age to talk to a girl. Grace didn't notice Amy until her third week there; Grace has always kept to herself—at home, on the playground, and, as she got older, at work.

Amy was on a swing by herself when Grace saw her for the first time from the monkey bars. Grace thought about leaving Amy alone, but she really liked the rain boots Amy was wearing, so she decided the girl on the swings must be someone great since she had great boots. Grace walked over to the swings, sat on the one next to Amy, and began kicking.

"Hi," seven-year-old Grace said, picking up height.

Seven-year-old Amy gave no reply.

"I really like your boots," continued Grace.

Still looking straight ahead, Amy replied, "Thanks. My mom picked them out for me."

"What store did your mom get them from? I would like a pair like them."

"I don't know. Do you want them?" Amy asked.

"Oh no, I can't take your boots," replied Grace.

"Here." Amy hopped off the swing, motioned for Grace to get off, and when she did, Amy took off her left boot. She told Grace to take off her left shoe, and after some hesitation, she did. Amy gave Grace her left boot, and in turn she took Grace's left shoe.

"I don't really understand," Grace said.

"You said you couldn't take my boots, so I only gave you one. Now we both have a boot."

The bell rang after a moment of the two girls smiling at each other. They somehow made it through the rest of the school day without their teachers noticing their mismatched shoes, but once they went home, both Grace and Amy got in trouble by their parents.

They have been inseparable—for the most part—since.

Amy takes another bite and smiles at Grace.

"What?" Graces asks.

Nothing. Just, the food tonight doesn't suck. And this beats the crap out of studying."

Grace gives a little laugh and goes back to her food. For a moment she loses herself in thought. Her chewing becomes rhythmic as her thoughts take her further and further from the cafeteria table. It's not uncommon for Grace to sneak away into her mind, and it often comes when Amy goes on a gossip tell-all.

Most of the time Grace's thoughts revolve around things such as items due on her calendar and figuring out her future. But sometimes, when she is in a particular mood, her mind will take her to thoughts and questions about life, death, and all that scary existential stuff that most of humanity tries to stuff into a little box and hide in the closet. But that stuff doesn't bother Grace. She enjoys it; the problem is, she doesn't have anyone to talk to about these questions and ideas she has, so for the most part she keeps them chained up in her cortex.

A few minutes pass before the silence is broken by two men talking as they walk up to the Grace and Amy's table.

"Hey, do mind if we sit with you two?" one of the guys asks, "All the other seats are taken."

Grace looks away from the two and around the cafeteria. She notices half the place is empty, and laughs. "Sure, you can sit with us."

The two men smile at each other and take seats next to Grace and Amy.

The one sitting next to Amy puts up a hand. "Hi, I'm Victor." Amy looks at him for a moment and then shakes his hand.

The other guy does the same to Grace: "Hey, I'm Henry." Grace smiles her genuine and infectious smile and then shakes his hand. Henry is instantly captivated.

◆ ◆ ◆

"Hey, bro, are you still awake?" Henry asks, lying in his bed.

Victor, on the other side of the room, in his bed, replies, "Dude, we turned off the light, like, five minutes ago. Who falls asleep that quickly?"

"My sister does sometimes. Or at least she did when we were young and shared a room. Maybe she doesn't now; I don't know."

Victor lets the room fill with a subtly awkward quietness. After a moment he says, "So what's up? Why'd you want to know if I was still awake?"

"What did you think of Grace and Amy?" Henry asks.

Victor looks up into the darkness, trying to see pass the black void and at the ceiling. "They seemed cool. I didn't talk to Grace all that much, but I saw that you did. Amy seemed really nice—and she even gave me her number, so that's cool."

Henry turns from his side onto his back. He berates himself internally for not getting Grace's number. He doesn't know why, but he feels a connection with Grace, even after only talking with her over some pasta and salad. He comes to the conclusion that he will most likely see Grace again around campus, and, if he really wants to see her, Victor has Amy's number, so it should be easy enough to get Grace's number through those means. Still, Henry scrunches his face in the darkness at the thought of not seeing Grace ever again. Sure, he doesn't know Grace, but that's why it would be so bothersome not to see her again: he genuinely wants to know her.

Victor sits up slightly in his bed, wondering why Henry hasn't replied. Victor knows that Henry is more of the quiet type, but Henry was the one to bring up the girls, so there must be something he wants to talk about. Just as Victor is about the speak up, Henry interjects:

"Yeah, they do seem pretty cool."

Victor gives a light chuckle and lies back down into his bed.

"Hey," Henry says, after a moment of silence.

"Yeah?"

"Isn't Grace beautiful?"

"That's a little weird, dude. I mean, yeah, she's hot, but we don't really know her."

"What do you mean?" Henry asks.

"Well, I don't really call a woman beautiful unless I know her. For a woman to be beautiful, everything about her must be beautiful: her personality, her attitude, her looks, even her soul. For all we know Grace is some stuck-up brunette with a foot fetish. So, for now, she's just hot."

Henry thinks for a moment. "That actually makes sense. But I talked to her enough to know she's not stuck up. I'm not sure about the foot fetish thing, though. But either way, I have good feet, so it doesn't matter."

Victor and Henry both laugh. The laughter makes the room appear less dark.

"All right, man, I'm going to bed," Victor says. "Some buddies want to do some batting practice tomorrow."

"Baseball doesn't even start until the spring. Why do you guys practice all the time?"

Victor, unbeknownst to Henry, scrunches his face. "Because we have to stay on top of our game. If I didn't pitch regularly, I wouldn't be as good. Practice is necessary."

"That makes sense," Henry replies. "Good night."

"Good night, man."

◆ ◆ ◆

Grace and Amy find seats toward the back of the lecture hall, as per Amy's request. If it were up to Grace, she would gladly sit in the front—not only to hear the professor better, but she also feels as though sitting in the front keeps her from distractions (one of those being Amy). Both of the girls are taking an introduction to logic course. Grace finds the class rather interesting, whereas Amy on the other hand, as she said the week prior, finds more interest in the gum under the desks—not that she would ever touch it, of course.

"Hopefully the professor doesn't show up today," Amy says with a smirk on her face.

"It's your tuition money," Grace laughs. As Grace puts her backpack next to her desk she sees Amy texting. "You've been texting since we got up this morning. Who is that?"

"Oh," Amy begins, still texting, "it's Victor. One of the two guys from the other night. He and... um... I think his name is Henry? Anyways, they both want to hang out with us soon. Like, sometime this week I think."

"That sounds like—"

Before Grace can finish her sentence, the door slams to their left, and the professor makes his way to the front of the class.

"Dammit," Amy murmurs.

The professor proceeds to take a marker out of his messenger bag and write on the board:

PROFESSOR THOMAS CRAMP

PSYCHOLOGY 130

The professor then turns around to the class. "Hello class. Yes, I know it is now October. But there are still students showing up who have not come to any of the previous classes, and therefore I find it necessary to make sure they know my name and class name," Professor Cramp lightly chuckles. "Sure, since they've missed a month of classes, and two quizzes, it'll be very difficult for them to pass this class with something better than a C. But hey, let's give them some false hope!"

Amy squints her eyes as Professor Cramp dives into the outline of the day's class. She slightly leans over to Grace and says, "Can we leave?"

Grace looks away from the front of the room and to Amy. "What? Why?"

"This class is boring."

"But you're a psychology major!" Grace whispers harshly.

"Yeah, but this isn't really psychology. Besides, it's not even one of my major courses. It's just a gen. ed. course for me just like it is for you."

Grace looks back to the professor in order to relieve her area of commotion. After only a few moments of hearing Professor Cramp speak, Grace is absorbed back into the lesson. She begins taking notes (the same notes Amy will eventually "borrow" in order to pass the midterm), and Amy grows restless after playing with her hair for only six minutes.

"So, Grace, do you want to hang out with those guys?"

"Oh, yeah. That sounds like fun," Grace whispers, still writing in her notebook.

"Don't sound too excited."

"What? I'm just trying to pay attention. I do think it'll be fun."

"Okay. So how does tonight sound?"

Grace stops writing and looks at Amy. "Tonight?" Grace asks.

"Yeah, I guess they're both free tonight."

"Then sure. That's fine," Grace says, and smiles at Amy.

Even though Amy has known Grace for years, she is still struck by Grace sometimes. Every so often, when Grace is being unknowingly and completely natural, she will do something that thoroughly takes Amy off guard. Even Amy has told people about Grace's beauty and elegance. Amy finds comfort in the fact that Grace has not recognized her true beauty, and, because of that, Amy never feels threatened or intimidated by Grace. That doesn't mean Amy sometimes feels out of place while walking along the street with Grace, or while shopping with Grace, but it does mean that she finds happiness in Grace's unending humbleness.

Grace stops smiling and goes back to taking her notes. Amy lingers for a moment, studying Grace as she thoughtlessly places her strong strands of hair behind her ear. After a moment, Amy recovers and goes back to her phone. She texts Victor a confirmation for the night, and sends him their dorm building and room number.

"There, I told Victor that we're good for tonight," Amy says, smiling.

"Good," Grace says, still taking her notes.

Amy lingers again for a moment, but this time on Grace's notes. She notices that in-between her note taking, Grace tends to draw flowers and scenic pictures—scenery such as a tree with mountains in the background, or a field of wheat with a windmill planted in the middle. Amy wishes to study these images more, but Grace looks up and notices Amy staring at her notes.

"What?" Grace asks.

"Oh, I was just looking at your little drawings," Amy replies, startled.

Grace grows embarrassed and covers her notes and drawings with her free hand and body. "Stop looking!"

Amy laughs.

"It's not funny," Grace whispers. "These notes and pictures are personal."

"Well, everyone behind you can see them if they wanted to."

"Amy, we're sitting in the back!"

"Oh yeah."

Grace quietly giggles, and Amy is struck once again.

Amy thrusts her entire body onto her bed. She grabs one of her pillows and presses it to her chest and wraps both her arms around it. She has a humorous thought that she may be hugging her pillow too hard, and that it is in pain because of the squeezing. She quietly giggles to this thought. After realizing she may have giggled a little too loud, she brings up her head and looks at Grace. Grace has stopped cleaning the dorm and is now staring at Amy. The two stare at each other for a moment.

Amy smiles at Grace. Grace gives a fake sigh and smiles back. Amy puts her head back onto her pink blanket and stares up at the ceiling. She begins pondering the idea of other worlds: *What if each piece of acoustic on the ceiling is a tiny world, and they're all inhabited by little creatures just like us? Is earth not just one piece of acoustic? Maybe there's a creature right now looking at the acoustic earth.*

Amused by this notion, Amy stands up on her bed and reaches up to the ceiling.

"What are you doing?" Grace asks suddenly.

"Playing God." Amy proceeds to pick a piece of acoustic off the ceiling. She crushes it with her thumb and index finger. "Destroyer of worlds."

"That's Death," Grace says. "Death is the destroyer of worlds. But maybe he's a god. I don't know."

"Whatever. I'm playing a powerful being. There."

Grace is about to get back to cleaning when she realizes that Amy isn't helping.

"Amy."

"What?" Amy is still standing awkwardly on her bed, losing her balance every few seconds.

"Can you please help me clean?" Grace asks.

"Why? It's just Victor and Henry. And besides, the dorm isn't really even dirty."

Grace sighs. "Please clean up some of your trash."

Amy lets her legs collapse, and she falls into her bed. "Fine."

Amy slowly and painfully gets out of her bed and picks up some scraps of paper off her desk. An ingenious idea to throw a wad of paper at Grace pops into her brain. And so she does it. The paper ball hits Grace right in the back of her head. Grace freezes mid-motion. Amy produces a wide smile that seemingly stretches from one ear to the other.

"Amy."

Trying not to laugh, Amy replies, "Yes?"

"I will absolutely *destroy* your world."

"What?" Amy loses her smile and grows a bit concerned.

"I am become Death, the destroyer of Amy!" Grace whirls around and throws both wads of paper that she has in her hands. Amy, completely caught off guard, takes both hits—one to the face, and the other to the neck.

"Hey!" Amy shouts after her initial shock. "How dare you? I am Death! I destroy worlds, not you! I was the one who crushed the piece of ceiling, not you. It is my rightful place to be Death. Are you, Grace, telling me that you wish to challenge me for the role of Death? Because, believe me, I will bring destruction and chaos into your simple existence."

Grace opens her mouth, but she finds herself unable to reply to Amy.

Amy smirks. "That's what I thought, peasant."

Grace stares at Amy for a moment. They both erupt into laughter.

After a few moments, and after their laughter has died down, a knock on the door is heard.

"Oh, that's probably them. You'd better hurry up and finish cleaning," Amy says.

Grace glares at Amy as she places an old wrapper into her trashcan. Amy sticks her tongue out at Grace, laughs, and then walks toward the door. Before answering the door, Amy, for some unknown reason to her, begins thinking about what Victor told her over text earlier: "Henry has been bringing up Grace a lot. I think he has a thing for her. He's never really had a girlfriend as far as I know, so tonight could get awkward between them."

So what if Henry does like Grace? Amy thinks, now gripping the doorknob. *Grace has never really had a boyfriend. She's too preoccupied with reading books and drinking her strawberry smoothies. She's way too addicted to those. Besides, I bet she hasn't really even noticed Henry.* Amy opens the door.

"Hey-o!" Victor shouts, with his hands in the air, once he sees Amy appear as the door disappears.

Amy smiles at him. "Hey, Victor!" She looks to Victor's left and sees Henry. "Hey, Henry." She smiles again.

Meanwhile, Grace is in the background fixing Amy's bed. Henry adjusts his neck and head so that he can see Grace behind Amy.

"Hey, Grace," Victor says over Amy's shoulder.

Grace looks up from Amy's bed. "Hello, Victor," she says, and smiles. She notices Henry looking at her. "And hello to you, Henry." Her smile is persistent.

"Come in," Amy says, and she moves her body out of the way.

Victor walks into the dorm, and Henry follows behind him. Victor immediately soaks in the presence of Amy, Grace, and

Henry, and he feels, all at once, comfortable in their company. Henry, on the other hand, is noticeably nervous; he has lost the knowledge of what his hands *should* be doing, so he has delegated one to playing with his lanyard, and the other to tapping on his thigh. His eyes are darting across the dorm, and he knows that if he tried to keep still he would shake. *Shit.*

Grace finishes with Amy's bed, and then walks over to hers. She sits all the way back on her bed, with her back against the wall. Over her right shoulder is a cute poster of a litter of kittens (Henry's now-favorite poster).

Amy walks over to her bed and sits on it in the same fashion that Grace has on hers. Victor takes the liberty of pulling out Amy's desk chair and setting it close to Amy's bed. Henry does the same with Grace's chair, but his movements seem somewhat awkward and unrefined. *Damn this nervousness.*

"So, what do you guys want to do?" Amy asks.

"We could just talk and hang out," Victor replies.

Grace finds this notion to be a tad weird. She and Amy just met these two guys a few nights ago. Why do they want to come over and just talk? But, since Grace is a naturally trusting person, she searches—and finds—the best in Henry and Victor. To her, they're just two guys looking for friends, and she and Amy seem to fit their qualifications—even though she didn't apply for the position.

"Well, if you want to hear me go on about something," Amy begins, "then I could talk about my critical thinking class. Grace and I are taking it, and it sucks! It's an early class, the professor is boring, and the material is dry."

"How would you know that the material is dry if you don't even pay attention in class?" Grace asks, trying to hold back a laugh.

Amy gapes her mouth at Grace. "Very funny! But seriously, you guys, this class is ridiculous. It's a waste of my time."

After a moment, Victor looks at Grace. "What do you think of the class, Grace?" he asks.

"Oh, well," she thinks for a few seconds. "I kind of like it. Sure, it's a little too early in the morning, but I find the information useful."

"Useful? How?" Amy abruptly asks.

"Well, it's helped me write in a more argumentative and logical way. Also, I can look at other people's writing and find fallacies easier. It's neat."

Henry leans forward in the chair. "I took a critical thinking class last semester. I don't think it was the one you're taking, but I found the class interesting as well."

"Wait; you're not a freshman?" Amy asks.

"No, we're sophomores," Victor replies, pointing his finger at Henry and then back to himself.

"Huh."

The evening soon turns into night, and the four college students had lost track of time hours ago. No one was checking their phones, and Amy's alarm clock somehow got knocked onto its face over the course of the night. The conversations jump from classes and professors and majors to desired careers and lost loved ones.

"I want to be a marriage counselor," Grace says sometime around eleven o'clock.

"I'm a psychology major. I don't really know what I'm doing yet," Amy says shortly after Grace finishes up her decision in wanting to be a marriage counselor.

Victor, unsure of what he wants to do, tells everyone that he has chosen liberal studies as his major. He assures the room, or perhaps himself, that it's just a placeholder for a real major that he'll choose soon. He also goes on to briefly mention that he had an older sister, Lily, who died of cancer when he was ten. This information changes the mood of the room, so he apologizes, and changes the subject to baseball.

Henry remains quiet most of the night, leaving Victor as the one to make them all laugh. Amy is the first to fall asleep, which happens around one in the morning. Victor is about to see if Henry wants to leave, but he sees that he and Grace are talking quietly. So, instead of leaving, he asks Grace for a blanket. He sets up a makeshift bed on the floor and lies down. He quickly falls asleep as well.

Grace tells Henry that she doesn't want to wake them up. Henry suggests that they could go out into the common area in the hall and talk for a bit. Grace smiles and agrees. Henry, just like many others have been, is stunned by Grace's smile. It's a weird experience to have, being touched by a mere smile. Henry thinks about this as they walk down the hall. Grace is a human just as he is. She has her faults, her imperfections, and she carries the weight of the regrets she has just like he does. But, perhaps, he thinks, her shoulders are broader than his, or maybe her regrets and burdens are lighter. But still, she is just a human. So why, then, is her smile so powerful? So extraterrestrial? To think that she doesn't belong on this planet is a ridiculous notion, yet here he is, about to sit down on a worn-out couch, thinking just that.

He wonders if Grace is even aware of all the snapped necks and heart palpitations she has caused. *Does she know that her smile causes her cheeks to fold just the right amount? Does she know her hair streams downward like a waterfall? Hell, does she even know how beautiful she really is?* Henry is in awe.

"You never said what your major is," Grace says, sitting next to Henry on the old couch.

Henry snaps out of his Grace-indulgent thoughts. "Oh, um, I'm an English major."

"Really?" Grace's eyes light up. "What do you want to do with your degree? Do you want to be a teacher?"

"Well, that's kind of, like, plan b, I guess," he says. "I actually want to be a writer." He blushes and looks away from her.

Grace lets the area fill with silence. She doesn't avert her eyes from Henry at all.

"I've been working on a couple poems, as well as some stories," Henry says, and looks back at Grace.

"Can I read some of your work?"

"I don't know. I only have a few things finished, and even then, they're not really finished."

"Please!" She implores, and grabs his arm.

Henry blushes again, inhibiting his thought processing. "Maybe I'll just write something new for you."

"Really? When?"

"Whenever I get inspired, I suppose."

"What inspires you?"

"A lot of things. Like, life itself, and the stars, and even slices of life."

"Slices of life? What do you mean?" she asks.

"Um, like, little episodes of life taken out from life itself and turned into words. But these writings—or prose pieces, as I call them—are typically saturated with descriptions and adjectives. They sound nice, but they're very impractical; that's why I try to keep them short."

"Those sound nice. I would like to read one of those."

Henry's red cheeks remain vibrant. "Ha, maybe."

After a moment, Grace says, "So why do you want to write?"

"I don't know. Well, I do know. I consider myself a creative person. I like creating things. But I want my writing to have some type of effect on people. Like I've told my mom before, I want my words to move the hearts of people, both physically and emotionally."

"Physically?"

"Um, you know how you can feel your stomach drop and heart sink sometimes? Like when something sudden happens?"

"Oh, yeah."

"I want it to be like that. I want my words to take people off guard, and have their hearts skip beats."

"Oh, I see. I really like that, Henry."

"Yeah. And I want to create worlds and universes that even God would compliment."

Grace soaks in his words.

"But we'll see. Maybe I'll just become a teacher," Henry laughs.

"No," Grace says. "I think you should really strive to write. What you've said is very beautiful. You should go for it."

"Wow, thank you, Grace."

Henry looks away from Grace and to the clock on the wall. Grace looks at the clock as well, and they both realize that it is getting pretty late. Henry stands up, reaches his hand out to Grace, and helps her up. They walk back to her dorm, and after getting inside, Henry quietly wakes up Victor, telling him it's time to go. Amy, being a light sleeper, wakes up and sees Victor walking out the door.

"Good night, Victor," she calls out.

"Good night," she hears his voice say from the hallway.

Victor trails behind Henry on the way back to their dorm. He's weary-eyed, and just wants to go back to sleep. But then Henry starts talking.

"Victor, Grace is amazing!" Henry exclaims.

"That's great, man. Amy's pretty cool too," Victor replies, rubbing his left eye.

"No, like she's really great. She told me that I should push for my dream of being a writer. I don't know; it's like, whenever she says something she says it with all her heart. Like she truly means it. It's genuine and touching. I don't know."

Victor yawns. "So, what, do you love her or something?"

"What? No!" Henry shouts. "I don't love her. But I think... I think I have feelings for her."

Henry's words wake Victor up a little bit. "Be careful, Henry."

"What do you mean?"

"Don't try to rush anything, or force anything, with her."

"I'm not, man. Don't worry."

Henry and Victor finally reach their dorm, and Victor walks directly to his bed and plops down onto his pillows, skipping the routine of undressing and brushing his teeth.

"Good night," Henry whispers.

Victor mumbles something inaudible, causing him to drool on his pillow.

◆ ◆ ◆

Grace throws a pillow at Amy's seemingly lifeless body, and shouts for her to get up. Grace doesn't want to be late—again—because of Amy. Sure, this is Amy's least favorite class, but the midterm isn't too far away, so Grace finds it logical to get to class on time. Amy throws a short-lived tantrum, and then slouches over her bed.

"I don't wanna," she mumbles.

Grace throws another pillow at Amy. Amy takes the pelt like a trooper, and offers no retaliation, which slightly aggravates Grace. Grace contemplates leaving Amy behind, thinking she really meant that she didn't want to, and subsequently wouldn't, go. But Amy surprises Grace by rising from her bed and walking over to her closet. Amy, for once in her life, thoughtlessly grabs a shirt from her closet, and then does the same for some pants from her dresser. Grace is taken aback, and wonders if Amy just shouldn't go to class.

"Oh yeah," Grace remembers, "Your text tone went off a little bit ago."

This perks Amy up. She rushes to her phone and unlocks it. After a moment of her eyes darting horizontally on her screen, her thumbs begin to blur.

"Who is it?" Grace asks.

Amy, without knowing, smiles as she looks up at Grace. "It's Victor."

"You two have been texting a lot since we hung out the other night. If I didn't know better—"

"It's not like that," Amy cuts in. "We just have a lot in common, and we connected well, and he's cool, and obviously I'm amazing."

"You're not helping your case, Amy."

"Shut up." Amy returns to texting.

Grace puts her laptop into her backpack. "Come on, Amy; we need to go."

Amy sighs. "I don't see the point. I heard the professor is moving anyways. Why couldn't he have moved before we got here?"

"It's not that bad, Amy. Stop being a baby. Now finish getting ready, lovebird."

"What?"

Grace kisses the air a few times.

"What is that supposed to mean?" Amy asks, sarcastically.

"That's you kissing Victor." Grace laughs. Amy picks up one of the pillows that Grace threw at her, and finally offers a retaliation. Grace gives out a quiet scream as the pillow hits her, and then she laughs even more. Amy eventually joins in on the laughter. A few moments pass, then Amy throws her clothes on, rushes to bathroom, brushes her teeth and hair, and then meets Grace in the hallway.

"So where did you hear that Professor Cramp is moving?" Grace asks as they wait for the elevator.

"I heard some of our classmates talking about it as we were walking out of class last night. I guess this is supposed to be his last year here."

"How long has he been here? He doesn't look old enough to retire."

"I don't know, and I don't care. Long Beach State will be better off without him."

Grace furrows her brows. "He really isn't that bad, Amy. Don't you think you're being a little harsh?"

"Nope," Amy says as they walk into the elevator.

Grace sighs, knowing very well that arguing with Amy never produces ripe fruit.

"So what are you and Victor talking about?"

"He wants to go get ice cream tonight after he gets done with practice."

"Oh, ice cream, huh?" Grace gets in Amy's face, smiling deviously.

"It's not like that, Grace! He just wants to hang out."

"Yeah, I'm sure," Grace says, unconvincingly.

"If anything, it's Henry who's interested in *you*."

"What?!" Grace is taken off guard. "That's... That's ridiculous. Even if, I only see him as a friend."

"Sure," Amy says, unconvincingly.

Not sure what to do in the now-awkward situation, Grace decides to press the first floor button again. The elevator still moves at the same speed.

"So, how were your classes today?" Victor asks Amy, scooping his spoon into his "Double Fudge Delight Chocolate Wonder" ice cream.

"Well, I only had that one critical thinking class today."

"Okay. So how was that?"

"I don't know," Amy says, staring at the ice cream on her spoon.

"What do you mean you don't know?"

"I was too busy texting you!"

Victor stares at her for a second and then laughs. "Well at least your distraction was a good one."

They both scoop some ice cream into their mouths. Silence is felt by both members of the party, and so Amy figures she'd better bring something up to keep away the awkwardness. She remembers Victor talking about his sister.

"So, Victor, the other night, when you were talking about your sister—"

"I don't want to talk about her."

"Why not?" Amy asks.

"It's just all-around not a good subject. Maybe some other time. Okay?"

"Okay."

The sun finishes setting in the distance, and Amy feels the silence fall even heavier this time.

"I'm sorry," she says, remorseful.

"It's okay." Victor smiles at her.

Amy takes another scoop of her ice cream and slowly brings it to her mouth. Victor watches her, and as she wraps her lips around the spoon, she looks up and makes eye contact with Victor. She feels vulnerable, and blushes; she looks away. Victor laughs a little, and continues looking at Amy.

"Stop," she whines, staring down at her ice cream cup.

"But I don't want to." The words shoot into Amy's ears like a needle thrust into an arm by an experienced nurse. Not only do

Victor's words take her off guard, but she clearly *feels* the meaning behind his words. The red in her face deepens, and so does the tightening in her chest. Her heart feels as though it's sinking, yet the beating grows more and more prominent. She wonders if her chest might explode, unable to hold back the adrenaline and nervousness coursing through her veins. Why is she so nervous?

Amy, by most people's standards, is above average. She's pretty, with a good height, and a solid personality. She's always found her nose to be her best feature, and others would agree. So, it should go without saying that she has had several relationship with guys who thought she was the bee's knees. She is not inexperienced when it comes to guys flirting with her, or growing close to her. So why is Victor making her so nervous? *Sure, he's a good-looking guy, and sure, he's pretty great, but my chest shouldn't feel like a pressure cooker.*

She forces her mind to quiet itself for a moment or two. She stares at her ice cream thoughtlessly. Then she lets her neurons fire up with beautiful, electric intensity. *Maybe there's a reason I'm feeling this way. Maybe this is a sign. Maybe, in all the vastness of the universe, the one I'm supposed to be with is sitting right beside me, eating chocolate ice cream. But that's absurd. I'm so young, and been to so few places. What are the odds that we would ever find each other? That is, if there even is such a thing as soulmates.*

"Dammit."

"What?" Victor asks, confused.

"Grace was right."

"Right about what?"

"Right about us. She basically said you and I have feelings for each other. Wow, she was totally right. I have feelings for you Victor."

Victor remains staring at Amy, but he blushes deeply, and smiles even deeper. "Thank God," he finally says, and puts his hand on hers, effectively stopping it from shaking.

"I'm surprised you didn't fall for Grace," Amy says nervously.

Victor laughs. "I fell from grace." He pauses. "Sorry, that was a bad joke. But no, You're the one that stuck with me after I met the two of you that night in the cafeteria. And you were the one I wanted to sleep next to the other night when we all hung out. Not Grace. You."

At this point, Amy is pretty sure her cheeks are about to catch on fire. She stares at him. He stares at her.

"So what does this mean?" Amy asks.

"It means that I'd better get that damn cuddle."

They both laugh.

"I'm sure that can be arranged," Amy says. "If you play your cards right. And if you don't turn out to be some kind of murderer or something."

"Okay, we'll take things slow. Damn, that sounds pretty cliché. But here: we'll finish our ice cream while talking about each other, and then, once both our ice creams are gone, I'll kiss you."

Oh great, here come the burning cheeks again.

Amy loses her composure for, like, a second, tops, and quickly straightens herself out. She stuffs her spoon into her mouth, forgetting the ice cream, and nods to Victor in agreement. He laughs. She blushes. Again.

Slowly, as their ice creams drain, and their grey matters fill with the knowledge of each other, Amy grows more and more assured that Victor truly is a nice guy. A wonderful guy, in fact. And she can see that he finds her to be just as amazing.

Victor stops talking and looks at their cardboard cups. He then looks up at Amy and smiles.

"What?" Amy asks, well aware of why he's smiling.

"Both of our ice creams are gone."

Amy nervously smiles and quietly says, "Would you look at that."

Victor stands up from his chair, straightens his shirt, and reaches his hand out to Amy. Amy places her hand into his.

"Where are we going?" she asks.

"I'm not going to kiss you in front of some ice cream shop. Geez, I'm classier than that."

Victor guides her by hand to a tree in the middle of a grass patch. The tree is ten yards from the ice cream shop.

"Much better. I can feel the romance in each blade of grass I step on," Victor says, drawing Amy closer to his body.

Amy allows herself to be moved by Victor, both physically and emotionally. She has never regarded herself as guarded, so it's rather easy for her to allow Victor the influence he currently has over her.

Victor brings his face closer to Amy's—to the point where their noses are touching. He stares into her eyes, and she stares into his. She isn't sure what he's seeing in her eyes, but she's seeing endless possibilities in his. No, endless realities, just like the acoustic on her dorm ceiling. And she is the decider of every single one.

And then they kiss under the shedding tree.

◆ ◆ ◆

Henry lies awake in his bed, continuously turning his body from one side to the other. After an hour or two or three of this restlessness, He finally tries to reach Victor. Victor is in the sleep realm, dreaming about the kiss he and Amy had shared earlier that evening. Or, at least, he *was* in the sleep realm.

"Victor. Are you awake?" Henry waits a few seconds. "Victor, are you awake?"

"I am now."

"Great. Good. So... How was your date with Amy?"

"I told you, bro; it wasn't a date." He smiles to himself in the dark. "Well, it wasn't at first. But I guess it technically turned into one."

Henry finds himself beyond intrigued. "Really? What do you mean?"

"Man, you sound like a girl asking about gossip." Victor laughs. "We kind of ended up realizing that we have feelings for each other. I mean; I kind of already knew that I did, but I don't think she knew at first. But we ended up kissing."

Victor thinks about that moment again. He is sure his brain has already moved it into his long-term memory storage, and he's grateful it has. He never wants to forget that moment, or the feelings that are tied to it.

"So are you two dating now?" Henry asks, hanging off the edge of his bed.

"I don't know, man. I would like to. Maybe. We didn't really talk about it." He pauses for a moment and thinks (this time not about the kiss). "I should probably ask her about that."

Henry laughs. They both allow the stillness of the night to fill the dorm once again. Now Victor finds himself turning from side to side, wondering what Amy is doing, and wondering if she is wondering what he is doing. *Does she want to be my girlfriend? Does she want a boyfriend right now? Damn, I shouldn't have talked to Henry.*

"Hey," Henry says.

"Yeah?"

"I have feelings for Grace," Henry says quieter than his sentences before.

"Really? Do you think she may like you?"

"I don't know. Like, she's been very encouraging about my writing and whatnot, and she's super nice to me. I don't know."

Still infatuated from his date, Victor says, "Bro, the only way to find out is to put yourself out there."

Henry hesitates. "I don't know if that's a good idea. I think I have some serious feelings for her. Like, I might love her."

This surprises Victor. "Whoa, are you serious? You don't even know her that well, man."

"I know; I know. It's just… It's like she saw the real me, and she really stuck with me after that night. I don't know. I'm just afraid that if I put myself out there, I'll get rejected, and I don't know how well I'll handle that."

Victor ponders this. Then he says, "Look, man; the only way to get anywhere in life, with anything, is to give whatever it is a shot. Just put yourself out there. I just hope you don't strike out."

Henry gives a soft laugh. "I hate your baseball references."

"It was pretty good, though, right?" Victor laughs. "So you'll do it? You'll see if Grace feels the same way?"

Henry sighs. "Yeah."

"Good! And maybe you'll get to first base with her."

"Shut up."

They both laugh, and then say good night to each other. Henry's mind races with all the possible outcomes that may come out of telling Grace how he feels. He doesn't sleep too well. Victor's mind races as he wonders if Amy wants to commit like he does. He doesn't sleep too well either.

◆　◆　◆

A week passes before Henry gains the courage to send a text to Grace asking if she would like to meet up. "Sure! We can get smoothies or something," her response reads. Henry reads her text as a good sign that she actually wants to hang out. They make plans to meet up that afternoon after he gets out of his final class for the day. All through his lecture on the different types of volcanoes present in California, He grows more and more nervous. *I should bail*, he thinks. *I shouldn't bail*, he thinks. He knows deep down that he is already committed to going through with it, so there's no point in truly trying to get out of it.

As class comes to a close he texts Grace telling her he is about to be on his way to the smoothie joint that is just off campus. "Okay. I'll see you there!" is her reply, with an added smiley face emoji. He takes this smiley face as a good sign. As he makes his way to "Smoothalicious," the knots in his stomach grow tighter and tighter until he believes that his stomach may have been hanged with a noose. Thank God he didn't eat earlier, as he would probably throw up right about now. And this makes him nervous about drinking a smoothie.

He walks into the smoothie place and sees Grace sitting alone with what looks like a strawberry smoothie on the table. He walks over to her, taps her on the shoulder, and says hi. She smiles at him and gets up to give him a hug. This takes Henry off guard. He takes this hug as a good sign.

"Are you going to get a smoothie?" she asks.

"Uh, yeah. I'll be right back."

"Okay," Grace says, and smiles at him.

Just like the emoji she used in the text, he thinks. He walks over to the counter and orders a banana smoothie. He stands awkwardly by the counter as the worker blends his smoothie, periodically looking over at Grace's back.

"One banana smoothie, my good man," the worker says as he places the order on the counter.

"Thank you," Henry replies. Henry walks back to the table and sees Grace staring at her smoothie. She giggles quietly. "What's so funny?" he asks.

"Oh," she starts, taken off guard, "nothing. I was just thinking about something that happened a few months ago."

"I see."

"What smoothie did you get? Banana?"

"Yeah. What gave it away? The color?"

"No, I heard the worker say 'One banana smoothie.'" She laughs. He laughs. He takes this as a good sign.

"Hey, do you want to go for a walk?" he asks.

"Sure."

Henry helps Grace to her feet, and they leave the smoothie shop. As they walk, they end up talking about Amy and Victor. Grace voices her opinion that she didn't think Amy was looking to settle down, yet here she is, in a relationship with Victor. Henry agrees, and remarks that it all happened so quickly. Grace nods her head, which causes the afternoon breeze to thrust her hair in her face. Henry laughs, and, with her hands, she brushes her hair out of her face, revealing a pouting face. Henry laughs even harder, and she quickly joins in.

They end up walking several blocks and finding themselves in El Dorado Park West. Only a couple hours of sunlight remain, so there aren't too many people present in the park. The tennis courts, however, are brimming with the local tennis club, so Henry and Grace decide to sit on a nearby bench and watch them play.

"Thanks for agreeing to hang out with me, Grace."

"Of course. You're really nice." Henry blushes, but not enough for Grace to notice. He thinks about the real reason he wanted to spend time with her, and he grows nervous. Flashbacks of being rejected by Janette Adams in high school shoot through his mind, and they scare him all the more. Henry places his hand in his pocket, and produces a folded up piece of paper.

"Hey, Grace," he says, and she looks away from the tennis courts.

"Yeah?"

He shows her the folded paper. "I wrote you something."

"Really?" she smiles, takes the paper, and quickly unfolds it. She reads:

At the end of the day, and once I am settled in with the thoughts of my soul (the same thoughts which seem to keep me from sleeping most nights), I have come to the conclusion about what I want from you, and what I want from us. I wish for our hearts no longer to be two separate systems, but instead two pieces reliant on the other in order to function. Perhaps your heart could be a boat, and mine could be a sail. Working together as one, my heart could guide yours, and your heart could give meaning to my existence, for without a sail a boat has no direction, and without a boat a sail has no meaning. I want my heart to be absolutely dependent upon yours. I want the blood that flows out of your heart to flow into mine. I want the same oxygen to be carried by the same blood. I want to meld into one with you.

-Henry

Henry watches Grace nervously as she reads his words that he wrote for her eyes only. He's certain that he even hears her sniffle once or twice, but her hair is blocking him from being able to see most of her face. After a few minutes she lowers the paper into her lap and looks up to Henry. Her eyes are watery. He takes this as a good sign.

"Henry, this is absolutely beautiful," she says, staring deeply into his eyes.

"I mean every word," he blurts out.

Grace looks surprised. "What do you mean?"

"What?" Henry feels slightly choked up.

"What do you mean you mean every word?"

"I mean that that's how I really feel about you, Grace, and what I want."

Grace realizes what Henry means. She looks away to the tennis courts.

"Oh," she finally lets out. "I'm sorry, Henry."

"Sorry for what?" Henry is realizing his fears are coming true, and there is absolutely nothing he can do to stop the ride now that it has started.

"I don't see you this way, Henry," she says, placing her hand onto the paper. "I don't want to be your boat. I'm sorry." Grace begins to cry. "I just... I just see you as a friend, and I'm really sorry."

"Well," Henry begins to say as a tear makes its way down his cheek, "do you maybe—I don't know—think you might see yourself having feelings for me someday?"

Grace wipes her right eye. "I don't know. I can't give an answer to that."

Henry stares at her for a moment. "Then I'll wait for you, Grace. I'll wait all through college, and then, if it hasn't happened by then, I'll come out here to this bench everyday and wait for you." The shaking in his voice is obvious.

Grace lets another tear find its way out of her tear duct. "I don't think that's a good idea. If you wait for me, I fear you may waste your time. Or worse. I don't want you to waste your life on me."

"It wouldn't be a waste if I ended up with you!" Henry says, raising his voice.

"Like I said, I don't know what the future holds for me. I just can't say anything besides that waiting for me would be a bad idea. And waiting on this bench is not a good idea either; you have my number." Grace gives a light chuckle to lighten the mood, but to no avail.

Henry stands up and walks around a little bit. "I'm going to do whatever it takes. And if that means coming out here everyday, then I'll do it."

"Henry, please."

Henry is at a loss for words. Grace stands up and motions that they should head back to campus. Henry complies. He doesn't take this as a good sign. The forty-five minute walk back was the most awkward thing Grace ever had to endure, and the most heart-wrenching experience Henry ever had.

Regret

"Well, can you stop? I haven't been talking to him, and I don't plan on talking to him. Robert's been calling *me*," Veronica said, folding her arms. She was seated in the passenger side of Tom's car, with her seat slightly lower than his. She didn't like this. It made her feel subordinate to him.

"Okay, okay. I believe you. I just think—maybe—you should change your phone number," Tom replied, treading lightly.

Veronica crinkled her nose and continued to look forward. The light had been red for some time now, and Veronica was growing annoyed. The heat coming through the windows, the air conditioner not doing its job; the light staying red for too damn long, Tom getting under her skin instead of under her nylons... It was all too much for her.

"I don't have to change my number. I like my number, okay? I have it memorized, and all my friends and coworkers have my number. I'm not going to change it just because you're insecure. Don't you trust me?" Veronica said finally.

"Of course I do. It's just... I mean; you left your husband for me. I don't know."

"Oh my God. You are not bringing your own trust issues into this." Veronica looked out the side window.

"That's not what I mean!" Tom put his hand to his forehead as he shifted to the left lane. "I just mean that you two have a lot of history together. It worries me."

Veronica relaxed her face and looked at Tom. "Don't worry. I left him for good reasons, and you know that. I came to you for good reasons. You know that." Veronica unfolded her arms and put her left hand on Tom's leg. "I love you."

Tom thought about asking if she still loved Robert, but he decided against it. Instead, he brought his hand down from his forehead and covered Veronica's. He looked at her, smiled, and felt, for a moment, at ease.

Tom never directly asked for any of this. He was visiting a close friend in some town that he always forgets the name of, and then, while visiting his friend's coffee shop, he saw a woman sitting alone at a bar that sat against the entrance window, with glasses carelessly placed on her bridge, engrossed in a play. Why would she be reading a play at a coffee shop on a Thursday morning? Remembering back eight months, he doesn't recall her wearing a wedding ring, as he believed he wouldn't have gone up to her if she had. But she wasn't wearing one, so he went up to her.

"Ah, *Sure Thing*. I read that play about fifteen years ago. If I remember correctly, it was good," Tom said nervously to the side of Veronica.

Veronica looked up and took in Tom's figure. "It's okay. Better than this coffee."

Tom laughed and looked back at the counter, hoping the workers didn't hear her. Obviously they were too far away, but he was nervous, so his frontal lobe wasn't working efficiently. After a moment of awkward eye gazing, Tom spoke up: "Sorry, my name's Thomas."

"I'm Veronica," she said, and put out her hand for Tom to shake.

"Mind if I sit with you?" he said after shaking her hand.

Veronica put the temple of her glasses into her mouth and let her teeth roll them as she pondered her answer.

She smiled. "Go for it."

Tom pulled out the chair next to Veronica, and sat on it, as one usually does with a chair. He looked out the window for a moment, and focused on a man sitting on a bench. He began wondering about this man's life, and this calmed his nerves enough to turn to Veronica. She felt his breath on her left arm, so she lifted her head away from her book and looked at Tom.

"What can I do for you, Thomas?" Veronica asked.

"Oh, please, call me Tom," he replied.

"Okay, *Tom*, what can I do for you? Would you like to read this play with me?" She chuckled slightly.

Tom's face reddened a smidgen, but his naturally tanner complexion masked it well. "No, I just saw you sitting alone, and you looked nice to talk to," Tom laughed nervously.

"Are you saying I looked lonely?"

"No, no. There's a difference between being alone and being lonely."

"Well, it would be a lie to say that I wasn't feeling a little bit of both," Veronica said, tracing the frame of her glasses.

"I'm sorry to hear that."

"Don't be sorry. You've played no part in my loneliness. Besides, you're helping right now."

Tom smiled, and this made Veronica smile. "I'm glad."

Tom and Veronica spent the next two hours talking about things that probably didn't really matter to either of them, but they found themselves to enjoy the other's voice and company, so they both rambled on about unimportant things. Since no topic brought up was particularly important, Veronica never mentioned her failing marriage, and Tom only realized this now in retrospect. And, since Tom didn't want to come off as a snob, he neglected to mention his tenured career at a university.

Obviously, they know all of these things—important and not—now, but that's only because Veronica happily gave Tom her number as he got up to leave the coffeeshop.

"No, park over there," Veronica said, pointing in front of her and to the right.

"Why not over there, in the other aisle?" Tom asked, looking out his side window.

"Because this spot is closer to the front, and I don't want to walk anymore than I have to in the heat."

"You're right." Tom moved forward a tad, and turned into Veronica's chosen parking spot. Veronica quickly got out of the car as Tom turned the key. This is normal for her, as she has never been able to stand the still heat inside of cars. She doesn't think she will ever be able to stand it, and she doesn't particularly want to. Tom got out of his car and looked over its roof at Veronica.

"What?" she asked, beginning to move.

"You look really pretty. That's all."

"I look old. Let's go; it's hot."

Tom made his way to the box office to pay for the movie tickets while Veronica continued walking toward the entrance. After Tom paid for the tickets, he went inside and found Veronica standing by the right hallway.

"Sweetie, our movie's down the other hall," Tom said softly.

"Okay."

"Do you want any popcorn or snacks?"

"No, I'm fine," Veronica said.

Tom felt his heart grow heavy for a moment, and he grew afraid that something may be wrong with Veronica. He thought about asking her about how she's feeling, but he ended up reaching for her hand instead. His left hand slid its way into her right hand, and his heart lightened. *Sometimes, speaking only clogs the arteries of feelings with words*, Tom thought.

Tom, never a married man (but a serial monogamous), did not possess the experience that he believed Veronica to have. He knew the feelings of love, and loss, and loneliness (for those who argue that loneliness is not a feeling, but rather a state: you lack emotional experience), but he always believed that some higher level of love and loss comes with marriage, and its possible failing. Because of this, Tom saw Veronica as someone with a deeper receptor for feelings, and this saddened him; he could not relate to her on levels that mattered the most.

Did Tom, in the eight months that they have been together, think about marrying her? Of course. He's a bit advanced in age, so settling down is overdue in his mind, but he has also thought about all that comes with marriage: the proposal, the possible rejection, the planning, the waiting, the expenses, the suffocating thought of two lives crammed into one... He has often wondered if he's been alone for too long, and if he's grown too accustomed to it.

"Which row do you want?" Veronica asked. They were now in the dim theater, with the screen playing local ads behind them.

Tom snapped out of his thoughts. "Oh. Um... It doesn't matter. The middle is fine."

"Okay," Veronica led the small trek up the stairs, and stopped above the row she wanted to enter. She motioned for Tom to go first. He entered the row. He walked to the middle of it, and sat down in a spot he found to be favorable. Veronica walked into the row and sat to his right.

Tom looked at her. "Could you sit on my left?" he asked.

Veronica looked puzzled. "Why?"

"It'd be more comfortable for me."

"All right, I guess."

Veronica got up and moved to the other side of Tom. Something felt off, or wrong, but she couldn't figure it out. She realized this was the first time she and Tom had been to the movies together. She looked at Tom as he went to hold her hand, and she remembered Robert. She remembered their movie trips—how they laughed, cried, and whispered together in the theaters. She remembered the change in their seating arrangements, and how Robert liked to trace his finger around her wedding ring. She remembered it all at once, and she felt it all at once.

She needed to talk to Robert.

"I'll be right back," Veronica said.

"Where are you going? The movie is about to start," Tom said, looking at her with a raised brow.

"I just need to use the restroom." Veronica made her way to the lobby and called Robert.

"Veronica?"

"Robert, hi. I, um, I don't know why I called you. I just, um, I just—"

"How are you?" he asked. This casual question overwhelmed Veronica, and so she cried.

"I'm okay," she said, wiping her cheeks. "I miss you, Robert."

"I miss you too, Veronica."

"I'm sorry for everything. I'm so sorry. You were so good to me, and I'm so sorry. You were my first love. I experienced so much with you." Veronica paused for a response, but she heard nothing. "Robert?"

"That makes me sad," he said.

"What does?"

"You saying I was your first love."

"I don't understand," she admitted.

"You've been my only love."

Veronica let more tears find their way down her cheeks. "I'm so sorry."

"I forgave you months ago. It's all right."

"I think I made a mistake," she said, covering half her face with her hand.

"I'm sorry you feel that way," he said. "Not all mistakes can be fixed."

"I don't want to live with this."

"I didn't want to live without you, but I've been forced to. I'm sorry."

"Robert, I——"

"I've got to go, Veronica. Happy early birthday," he said, and hung up.

Veronica sat down in the lobby for a second and cleaned her face with napkins from the bin on the table next to her.

"You're just in time; the last preview just finished," Tom said as Veronica sat down.

"Okay."

Veronica stared at the screen, as one watching a movie probably should, and the brightness helped in the pursuit of her eyes tearing up. She felt a tear roll down her left cheek, and she wiped it away just as she had wiped Robert away: thoughtlessly and harshly.

Water

"Please tell me about Lily."

"Why?"

"Because you've only told me little things about her. I want to know her."

"What do you want to know?"

"Her."

"What about her death?"

"Yes."

Lily seems somewhat mythic in my mind now. It's been so long, so my thoughts of her have snowballed down the mountain of years. But she was a wonderful sister. She always seemed to have things figured out. I never felt afraid to ask her a question because I knew she would know the answer. I remember one time I wanted to see if I could stump her, so I asked her how fast a penguin could swim.

"Up to twenty miles an hour," she said, and stuck her tongue out at me.

She was very pretty for a sister. Of course, I was only ten when she died, so I wasn't too much into women, and she was also my sister. But our parents always called her beautiful, and I heard a couple of her guy friends call her hot a few times. My memories have her with shoulder-length blonde hair, but her pictures in my parents' house have her hair much longer, so I'm not sure which point in time my memories are from.

Lily had very nice teeth—I remember that. Our mom always said, "Lily, you have such beautiful teeth. It's almost as if you got them from me."

She did. Most definitely, Lily got her teeth from our mom. I, on the other hand, got my teeth from our dad. But, as you can see, my teeth are fine. They're just plain.

Lily had very green eyes. They looked nice with her blonde hair. As for height, she was about 5'6" or 5'7"—I remember the doctor reading one of those off her chart early on. Her height helped her in basketball. She played for her high school. I don't remember if she was any good, and our parents never talk about it. I know I went to a few games, but I don't really recall seeing her play.

One thing about Lily that no one knew, or knows, is that she had a diary. I saw her scribbling in it one evening, and she quickly hid it from me. After she died, I found it under her hamper in her closet. I still haven't opened it. I still dream about her sometimes, and I still dream about the day she died.

It was March 27th when Lily was diagnosed with ovarian cancer. More specifically, she had stage four invasive epithelial ovarian cancer. I was ten and she was sixteen. They say it's extremely rare for teens to get ovarian cancer, and for her to have progressed to stage four so quickly. People say a lot of things, but most of it doesn't mean shit. She got ovarian cancer, and she was stage four before being diagnosed. So explaining to our family that it was extremely rare didn't make things better.

Our parents took her to the doctors because she complained of abdominal pains for a couple weeks, and because she was constipated. My mom had to define the word "constipation" to me, and then she had to sit me down and make me stop laughing at the fact that my sister couldn't crap. I always hated the drive to our doctor; it was a forty-minute drive, and we went to him because he was a "family friend," even though I had never seen him in our home.

So there I was, in this dull, beige waiting room, complaining about having to be there. It's all kind of a blur, but a week or two passed before our mom received a call for them to return to the doctor's office. That's when Lily was diagnosed. That's when she was told she had about a fifteen-percent chance of living for five years. She died seven months after her diagnosis.

Initially, it was determined that Lily's cancer had spread to her abdomen and left lung, but it was later discovered in her bones as well. I say "Lily's cancer" as if she owned it, but it owned her. We had been directed to a hospital closer to our home, and the doctors there made a plan to treat her with chemo, then surgery, and then chemo again. They said her abdominal pain was coming from an obstruction, so they put a tube in her stomach to prevent her intestines from being overly blocked. I cringed every time I saw the tube coiling out from under her blanket like some venomous snake digging into her existence.

The last few months were, obviously, the hardest. After they opened her up, the doctors discovered just how much of the cancer had spread, and their hopes for her dwindled. The doctors advised for her to stay in the hospital after she grew worse, and our parents complied. I thought then that she should have been at home her last month. I still think that. But Lily became friends with the nurses, and she had a certain attitude toward life that I think both perked the nurses up, and made them sad. But when things got really bad, and it turned out to be her last two weeks alive, was when I decided that spending time with her in the hospital was more important than going to school.

◆ ◆ ◆

"Victor, come here," Lily said, her voice quiet and coarse.

"What is it?" I asked as I walked closer to her bed.

"I need you to answer a very serious question."

"Sure," I replied.

"Do I look good bald?"

I looked at her and threw my arms up. "Come on!" I shouted, and walked back to the chair in the corner of her room.

Lily giggled, and then coughed. She always coughed. It disrupted her laughter just as December 26th disrupts the hanging of Christmas lights. She looked over at me and smiled, her chapped lips cracking with mini fault lines. I smiled back, looked away, and cringed.

"Where's mom?" Lily asked.

"I don't know. I think she went to the bathroom."

"I've told her to use mine."

"Yeah, but she doesn't like us hearing her go," I said.

"But we could hear her at home," Lily said.

"Well, yeah, but she doesn't know that." We both laughed, but Lily ended with a cough.

Lily's hospital room was white, and cold, and void of connections to her life. Her flowers that were brought in from friends were dying near her room's single window. Her bathroom door, on the opposite side of the room from her bed, was light brown, and other side of it there was a leaky sink faucet. Lily confided in me that it kept her up at night. "Well, either the water dripping, or my thoughts of dying," she told me.

She was placed on the fourth floor of the hospital. Apparently most people in the rooms on that floor were deemed to die, so my parents began calling her floor the waiting room. They told me this years later. Lily found herself to be alone half the time. We usually arrived around nine in the morning, and would leave around seven or eight at night. My mom would stay the night with her sometimes.

One time, when our parents left me alone with Lily, I gathered enough courage to ask her some insensitive questions.

"Lily," I said.

"Yes?" She replied, still looking at the cream-colored page of a book.

"Are you afraid of dying?"

She looked as if she were thinking for a few moments. "Hm. In my dreams I'm afraid. But it doesn't seem so bad while I'm awake. But maybe that's a coping mechanism."

"What's a coping mechanism?" I asked.

"It's something that people use to feel better about stuff," she informed me.

"So then how is that a coping mechanism for you?"

"Um… Maybe having those dreams about death helps me cope with it."

"Oh," I said, and looked at the ceiling. "What will you miss the most when you die?"

"I'll miss the same stuff you'll probably miss when you die: my family, my friends, my freedom. But I don't think I'll really miss all that, since I'll be dead. I'll be gone."

"Oh."

The hospital room grew quiet, and I kind of felt like crying.

"Hey," she said, breaking the silence.

"Yeah?"

"I've been thinking a lot about water."

"What do you mean?" I asked.

"Well, after spending a lot of time being pretty dehydrated, I came to realize just how essential water is. Like, we need it to have life. Just like we need death to have life."

"I don't get it," I said.

"Okay. Um. The only reason we have a word for light is because darkness exists, right? That's the same for good and evil. We have terms for them because the other exists."

"Okay," I said, confused.

"So, in order to *really* know what life is, we must have death. Otherwise life would just be the only thing we are. And that's no fun. That keeps us from understanding."

Ten-year-old me didn't understand what she meant, but I do now. Her obsession with water really went over my head at the time, though.

"But water," she began, "water is everything. They say we started out in water, and eventually crawled out of it. John F. Kennedy said—"

"Oh, he was a president!" I interrupted.

"That's right," Lily replied, and coughed. "He said once that he thinks we're connected to the ocean because that's where we came from. He said we're tied to it. I think that's beautiful."

"Me too."

"And some people die in a similar way to how the ocean is."

"What do you mean?" I asked.

"I mean that some people die like waves. Like, some deaths are as peaceful and calm as a wave rolling across the beach. Where other deaths—painful deaths—are like waves crashing against rocks and hill walls."

"Oh." I thought for a moment. "Which wave will your death be?"

"Well, my cancer is pretty painful, and I don't think I'll have the pleasure of quietly slipping away in my sleep. I think I'll end up crashing against the rocks."

"I don't like that," I said, and teared up.

"Neither do I," Lily said. "But I also don't like this cancer. I think it'll be a nice change of pain when I crash like a wave. And then all my pain will be gone."

I looked away from her as the tears spilled over my eyelids. She put her arm over her bed and touched my shoulder.

"Your tears are salty, just like the sea," she said as I looked at her.

"Stop," I cried.

"I'm sorry," she said calmly.

We stared at each other for a few seconds. She wiped my right cheek as I scrubbed my left. She coughed into her other hand.

"The surgery didn't do much," she said. "And the chemo hasn't helped."

"I know, but—"

"You're going to be such a great person, Victor. I can feel it. You might as well be the ocean itself."

More tears spilled onto my face, and I saw her eyes welling up.

"I love you so much, little brother, and I'm so sorry I won't be there to see you grow. You're my favorite person."

"You're my favorite person, too," I replied, choking on my mucus.

A tear rolled down her pale, sunken cheek. She looked up at the white ceiling and smiled solemnly. "I'm glad."

As you could imagine, her last few days were very gray and unhappy. She slept a lot then, and was very quiet when awake. I think we all knew her end was near, but our parents went full pseudo ignorant. Lily stayed quiet on the subject, but her defeated demeanor was as readable as a young adult novel. Our parents began finding excuses to step out of Lily's room, and the gray atmosphere pressed on my mentality. I hated being in that room, and I hated seeing Lily like that, but I needed to be there for her, and I loved her.

The day before Lily died, she smiled too much. It made me feel guilty for some reason, and I know it hurt her because of how dry her lips were. Her teeth were yellowed and her gums had receded. She no longer had her mother's smile; she no longer had her freedom.

I almost didn't go see her that day. My friend wanted to have a slumber party for his birthday, and my mom assured me that I deserved to spend time with my friends. But I thought of Lily's smile, and I grew guilty. I told my friend that I needed to see my sister. He said he understood, but he still seemed mad. I ended up going to school that day, and so after school I went to the hospital with my dad. Seeing her smile so much told my heart that she was leaving us. She was going to crash.

"Victor, I'm so happy to see you!" she said. "I have something for you."

"What is it?" I asked.

"Come here."

I walked up to her bed and watched her open up the drawer to her left. She showed me a picture.

"I drew this last night." It was a picture of the sun setting over the ocean. Birds were flying near some cliffs to the right, and a kite was flying on the bottom left edge. I still have the picture hanging in my dorm.

"It's very pretty," I said.

"I drew it for you. You see: I figured that you're actually too great to be the ocean. So I made you to be the sun. I can settle for being the ocean."

I heard my mom begin to cry behind me. I wanted to stay strong for Lily, so I fought the feeling under my eyes. "I love it, Lily! Thank you," I said, shaking as I took the drawing from her.

Our parents and I decided to stay the night that night. Have you ever seen *Good Will Hunting*? In that movie, Robin Williams says visiting hours didn't matter to him when his wife was dying; that's how it was for us. Lily slept peacefully that night, but our parents and I did not. Throughout the night we heard her breathing grow fainter.

As the sun began to peer through her window, she opened her eyes for the last time.

"Good morning," she said, smiling.

"Good morning," our dad said.

She glanced at each of us, first our dad, then our mom, and then me.

"How did you guys sleep?" she asked.

"Just fine," our mom replied. She walked up to Lily's bed and touched the rail.

"Be careful. The rail is always cold."

"It's okay," our mom said.

"I know. It's okay."

The sun found its way to Lily's face. She closed her eyes and smiled.

"It's warm," she whispered.

The white room was void of all sound besides that of our collective breathing. Lily's breathing became more shallow, as if the low tide were setting into her soul, the waves slowly pulling back from the shore. We all held our breath as we heard Lily's fade away. And like a wave of water gently washing over fine grains of sand, and then taking some with it, death washed over her, and washed away her existence.

Pebbles

Garrell Willis

"Some people, in terms of love, are colorblind" was Henry's favorite line that he had ever written, and it came from his first bestseller *Colorblind*. The title of his book clearly came from this line, and it took him all of ten minutes to write out the page-long argument that his protagonist makes regarding this statement of people being colorblind. And it took him all of two months to write *Colorblind*. He never intended for it to sell very well, or well at all, but it turned out that lonely, middle-aged women agreed with Henry (or rather his fictional characters). So that was how he found his audience.

Henry, aware of his audience and what they wanted, was now on the research side for his next novel. He decided that he deserved a little bit of relaxation, so he made his next novel to be set in Paris. Now he would have to go spend some time in and around the Eiffel Tower, gaining knowledge of the city for his novel as well as eating baguettes and drinking coffee. Henry had a fair amount of money from his three published novels and his one published anthology of short stories, so, financially speaking, Henry had no problem staying in Paris for three or four weeks.

The one problem that he did have in leaving was finding someone to watch his six-year-old Shiba Inu. His mother had said no; his sister made up some lame excuse about being in love with a cat owner; and his now-ex girlfriend went back on her agreement after they, well, broke up. As a last resort, he asked his elderly neighbor. His neighbor, a huge fan of his, said she would be honored to watch his dog, and then asked for his autograph.

Being a thirty-seven-year-old bachelor made Henry feel awkward around his neighbors. He still lived in a townhouse apartment, but the tenants around him all seemed to either be married, in a relationship, or widowed. Everyone in his complex thought of him as "Henry the author." This bugged him, so he decided to label some of the neighbors similarly: George the creep, Betsy the nurse, Ryan the bald, and so on. He disliked the fact that one aspect of his life was his defining characteristic to others, so he did the same to them; he boiled their existences down to one word. *This simplification dehydrated one's humanity,* Henry thought. He was more than an author. He was a brother; he was an amateur tennis player; he was a man living with an unfulfilled heart; he was a night owl.

Life slowed down at night, and things seemed to happen more slowly. Henry welcomed the moon and the stars just as blank pages welcomed his words. It was all so beautiful to him—the way the moon shone lightly on the trees and the roads, but still allowing for darkness in every crevice. He took these elongated nights to build worlds and create lives. But he never felt God to be completely satisfied with his creations, and this may have played a part in his heart being unfulfilled.

"Thank you again for watching Juhi, Martha," Henry said.

"It's no trouble at all," Martha replied.

Henry began walking toward the sidewalk. The taxi he called for an hour earlier had arrived, and he didn't want to be late to the airport. He heard his dog bark, so Henry turned around.

"Bye, baby!" he shouted. "Oh, Martha," he remembered, "can you please watch my car as well?"

"Sure thing, Henry."

"Thank you." Henry met the taxi driver by the trunk of the car and the two of them loaded his luggage. He got into the backseat and waved to Martha and his dog as he drove off. He put his arm back into the taxi as it rounded the corner. He sighed.

"Where are you going?" the driver asked, effectively overpowering the sound of the wind coming in from the window.

"Paris," Henry said, rolling up the window.

"Oh, I love Texas."

"No, no, France," Henry said, laughing.

"Oh! Excellent. I've always wanted to go."

"I'll send you a postcard," Henry laughed.

The rest of the ride to the airport was like most taxi rides: uneventful. Los Angeles traffic was Los Angeles traffic: eventful. The taxi driver informed Henry about the back-up on the freeway, and about their estimated time of arrival. Henry sighed and returned his vision to outside his window, where he could clearly see the traffic. The sun's reflection off the car next to him caused his mind to spiral into a weird thought of kids being reflections of their parents. Their parents instill in their children their own morals, ideas, and beliefs, and they also pass on their genetics. So, Henry thought, do parents really *instill* all these notions into their children, or do they *install* them, as if their genetics are just strings of code, and the parents are adding to that code?

Henry, within the cave that he resides in, which is in the side of the mountain made out of his nights alone, has thought long and hard about the possibility of life—all of life—merely being a computer simulation. He read about it online one night, and has thought about it a hundred nights since. Déjà vu? Simply glitches in the simulation. Shallow people lacking personalities? Characters created rather quickly—unnecessary additions to the simulation. Henry could probably talk about this "possibility" for a good amount of time, but no one would want to listen to such nonsense, so he has never brought it up in any conversation. So these thoughts remained in Henry's head, uncriticized by his ex, the taxi driver, and everyone else, whether long-term or momentarily, in his life.

A honk close to the taxi snapped Henry out of his thoughts. He cleared his throat and reached into his bag. After fishing for a moment he produced a glasses case. He opened the case; took out a pair of glasses; and introduced them to his face. He reached into his bag and took out his trusty, and worn-out, journal. He cracked ol' faithful open and reviewed some of his newest entries. These entries revolved around the plot and character developments for his latest novel.

"'Setting: Paris, France,'" Henry whispered.

The taxi driver heard Henry say something, so he looked in his rear view mirror and saw Henry reading to himself.

"'Time Period: Present-day.' Whatever the hell that means. 'Characters: Three male, three female.' Okay, yeah, I still want that."

Henry took his pencil from the crease of his journal and underlined the character count. "'Character names: Undecided.'" Henry thought for a moment. "I still don't know if I want the characters to be strictly American, strictly French, or a blend of the two. The names rely on this decision."

"Is everything okay, sir? You seem a bit irritated," the taxi driver said. This broke Henry's concentration.

"Yeah, yeah, I'm fine. Just thinking," Henry replied. He looked back at his journal. "I'll figure it out once I'm there." Henry sighed. Henry sighed a sigh fitting for someone of Odysseus' stature. Thirty-seven looked good on Henry, but living a life where love had consistently alluded him had caused him to think about how it will all eventually weigh down his scale. Henry, in that moment in the taxi, for no identifiable reason, felt his side of the scale sink a minuscule amount. He sighed again, but this time there was an earthquake in his chest, and the vibrations found their way out through his breath. *The world is heavy sometimes*, Henry thought. He was well aware that many knew this better than he. Atlas came to mind. Henry sighed again.

"Sir, the traffic is clearing up. It shouldn't be too much longer until we get to the airport."

Henry closed his journal and thanked the driver. Henry closed his eyes and tried to think about all the good in his life: his publications, the lives he has touched, and his dog. He smiled gently to himself in the backseat of a white taxi that was stuck in traffic. Henry thought about his ability to jump on a plane and spend some time in Paris for "research" for a new novel that he knew would sell quite well, and he thought about the countless nights that he has driven to the nearby mountains to spend time on the hood of his car and gaze up at the stars. He has become friends with many lights in the Milky Way.

But Henry is a romantic. And romantics, for whatever illogical and evolutionarily disadvantageous reason, pine for human connection. Dogs always do their best for people, and Juhi is living proof of this, but for humans there has to be more.

Henry sought more. He sought more in high school, in college, and even in most buildings in Chicago during his short stay there about ten years ago. There were times where Henry was content with his life (usually after receiving a check with a nice sum of money or reading a nice review of his works), but there were other times where Henry craved love and communication (usually after listening to Mumford and Sons or talking to the stars for hours with no reply). His most recent break-up has not helped remedy the metaphorical palpitations of his heart.

But even in seeking more, it is important to be grateful and appreciative for what is already in one's possession, and this is something that Henry struggled with. Henry was always looking for more, and never at what he already had. Or, rather, he was always looking at the one thing he knew he could not have.

"Pebble." Henry let this word quietly slip out from the confines of his thoughts. He looked up from his lap and out the window to his right. He was in front of the airport entrance.

"Sir," the taxi driver began. "We are here. I will grab your luggage for you."

"Thank you," Henry replied, still staring out the window. Henry shifted his thoughts to the notion of being stuck on an airplane for nearly eleven hours. Henry sighed once again, as discontent people tend to do, and began putting his journal and other small belongings into his bag. He opened the door of the taxi and got out just as the driver pulled out his last piece of luggage.

"Here you go, sir. Even with the traffic we made it in fair time. I hope you have a safe trip," the taxi driver said.

Henry pulled out his wallet. "Thank you for the ride," Henry said, and handed him a fifty dollar bill on top of his cab fee.

"Sir, you handed me too much."

"No I didn't." Henry smiled.

◆　◆　◆

After getting through the security line that followed like a tedious argument, Henry found himself in his terminal lobby. As expected, he was over an hour early for boarding, so this gave him ample time to sit down and begin brainstorming some plot lines for his novel. However, now standing in the lobby and looking around, he realized he could pass several hours on the plane doing this instead.

A few seats by some giant windows were vacant, so Henry chose the one closest to the window. He pulled out his phone to see if he needed to plug it in to charge; it was at ninety-five percent, as he had hardly touched it. He had no notifications. One word his neighbors would never associate Henry with would be "popular." Henry seldom had friends over, and he rarely left for more than an hour or two (depending on traffic) at a time, indicating to his neighbors that he was not out seeing people, but rather shopping or getting some coffee. Some of his neighbors believed fame had gotten to him, as they could sometimes see the stacks of mail he carried into his apartment from time to time. The truth of the matter was that Henry preferred to keep to himself. He kept in contact with a few friends from college, and one or two from high school, but other than them, he mainly kept in contact with himself.

The only reason he began dating his now ex was because she had recognized him at some coffee shop in a small town he went to in order to get out of the city for a bit and find some new inspiration. She impressed him with her nervous ramblings of various themes that she had found in *Colorblind*. His stomach now sank each time he thought about how nervous and excited she was when she first met him compared to her cold and distant demeanor when breaking up with him. The feelings seemed like a dichotomy, yet they arose from the same human.

Henry looked away from the window that was to his left and looked to the openness of the terminal lobby. He saw an older man walking toward him.

"Mind if I sit with you?" The stocky senior asked. He had a British accent and a gray mustache.

Henry looked around to the many open seats both near him and in the other parts of the lobby. "There are plenty of seats, but sure," Henry said.

"I know. But I'd like to sit next to someone."

"Are you going to Paris too?" Henry asked as the old man sat down.

"Yes."

"Then you'll be sitting next to someone for hours."

"And I look forward to that too." The old man smiled.

Henry was slightly taken aback. "Good for you. Well, I'm Henry."

"I'm Augustine," the old man said, and brought his right hand over his body for Henry to shake.

Henry shook his hand and then looked down at his own lap for a few moments.

"Why are you going to Paris?" Augustine asked, causing Henry to look at the old man. Augustine was wearing a light blue button up with thin white stripes. His pants were a medium brown, and were accentuated by his brown suspenders. *Yeah, he's old*, Henry thought.

"I'm going to do some research for a book I'm writing. It's going to be based in Paris, and I'd much rather be familiar with the city."

"You're a writer, eh? Are you published?"

"Yes. I've published a few books and a collection of short stories. I don't know if I'm that popular in England, though."

"Oh, I've lived all over," Augustine said. "I've lived in the US for the past three years. Before that, I lived in Denmark for a couple years; Egypt before that, and so on. I haven't lived in the UK for a long time, although I do go visit, of course."

"How do you afford to travel and live in other places?" Henry felt a little intrusive after asking the question.

Augustine chuckled. "I'm a retired man who made good decisions in this life."

This resonated with Henry. "I see."

"What about you? Are you paying for Paris with your book funds?"

Henry smiled and lightly laughed. "Yeah, bound papers with words on them are surprisingly valuable."

"It's the words that are valuable, Henry. Your words."

This surprised Henry. "Thank you" is all Henry managed to say.

"Don't thank me. Thank your parents or God or whomever you think shaped you into the writer you are," Augustine said while brushing his mustache with his thumb and index finger.

"What's taking you to Paris?" Henry asked, almost forgetting that Augustine was going the same way.

"I'm thinking about spending a month or two or three there, and then head back to Brentwood, my hometown, and see some family for a bit. So, just pleasure, as that will be my reason for everything I do in the coming years."

"That sounds nice," Henry said, partially to himself.

"It is. As was spending time in other places. Actually, living in Egypt is why I now sit next to people like you in public."

"How's that?" Henry asked.

Augustine thought for a moment. "Let me ask you: if you got on a bus, and there was one person sitting in the front, and one sitting in the back, where would you sit, Henry?" Augustine skimped on pronouncing the H in Henry's name each time he said it.

"I'd probably sit in the middle of the bus," Henry replied.

"As would most Americans. And most Brits. But in Egypt, they believe that no one should have to be alone. So if you were in Egypt, and that were you sitting in the front or the back, and someone walked on the bus, that person would sit next to you. That way you wouldn't be alone. I found myself in the company of many wonderful people during my time there, whether it was on a bus or in a bar."

"So why did you sit by me?"

"You looked lonely, and I felt lonely," Augustine smiled. "So I thought I could fix both our problems."

Augustine's reply struck two chords with Henry: one of annoyance, but another of understanding. Perhaps he was annoyed at the fact that Augustine, and probably other people as well, could tell he was lonely just by looking at him. But Henry understood. Augustine understood, too; that's why he sat next to Henry.

"Are you married?" Henry asked after a minute of silence.

"I made many good decisions in my life, but I also made bad ones. I have loved, and I have been loved, but I have hurt, and I have been hurt. Marriage, at one time, was a close and realistic concept to me. But things change; people change. I changed. It's all very vague—I apologize. In short, no, I am not, and have never been, married."

Henry found himself at a loss for words. The way Augustine spoke was borderline poetic, and it made Henry feel more connected to the universal theme of loneliness.

"Is that why you feel lonely?" Henry asked.

"Could be," Augustine replied. "I'm not sure. I'm seventy-six years old and I still haven't figured out how to calm the restless jellyfish in my heart."

"Jellyfish?"

"Yeah. I find that the thought of a jellyfish swimming around in my heart, brushing my walls with its tentacles, is a good representation of my feeling of loneliness. It might not suit you, but no one ever said loneliness feels one certain way."

"That's true," Henry agreed. He thought about the jellyfish, and began to feel a jellyfish swimming in his own heart. "I feel it too."

"Feel what?" Augustine asked.

"The damn jellyfish."

"Write about it."

"What?"

"Just give me credit."

Henry looked at Augustine and they both laughed. "Will do."

Augustine shifted in his seat.

Henry fiddled with his fingers. He felt the silence bring itself down upon them, but no loneliness tagged along as it usually had in Henry's countless encounters with silence.

"It's funny," Henry began. "Talking to you has put me somewhat at ease. I don't really feel anxious or lonely at the moment."

"That's because you're not alone in your loneliness." Augustine smiled and looked away. He looked up at the ceiling of the airport. "At least, you're not alone in your feeling of loneliness. We bear the weight together."

Henry felt calm. With the conversation between him and Augustine, and the brief intervals of quiet, Henry came to find himself calm for the first time since he read the first critic review of his short stories. Henry sat in silence next to Augustine for a few more moments and then stood up.

"I'm going to go to the bathroom," Henry said, straightening out his shirt.

"The what?" asked Augustine.

Henry didn't understand Augustine's confusion.

"Where are you going?" Augustine spoke up again.

Henry looked at him. "Oh! I'm going to the 'loo.'"

Augustine laughed, and his stomach rose and fell with his convulsions. "I'm only teasing, mate."

Slightly embarrassed, Henry chuckled a little and then made his way across the terminal lobby to the restroom. As it typically is for a men's restroom, there was no line. Henry always wondered why women did not just go into the men's restroom instead of wait-ing in line. He had argued internally before that no guy would real-istically care if a woman did such a thing. *Maybe they're afraid of being groped or harassed by men in the restroom*, Henry thought once. *Maybe at a bar that might happen. Women shouldn't go into a men's bathroom at any bar.* But he never saw a problem with it potentially happening at a restaurant. But even then, none of it really mattered; it's just a restroom.

The restroom did not smell too pleasant, but it smelled like what an airport restroom ought to smell like in Henry's mind. He walked over to a urinal and did his business. Two men walked in during the process, and, as it goes, none of the three paid any attention to each other. Henry washed his hands and exited the restroom.

"I watched your bag for you," Augustine said as Henry approached their seats.

"You're too kind," replied Henry.

Augustine combed his hair with his hand. "Henry, are *you* married?"

"No, I can't say that I am," Henry said sullenly.

"But you've been in love?"

Henry fiddled with his fingers. "I like to think so."

"When?"

"I guess college," Henry said dryly.

"What happened?" asked Augustine.

Henry looked down at his lap and noticed his fidgeting finger-ings. He calmed them and thought. "I loved a pebble."

Augustine furrowed his eyebrows. "What does that mean?"

"The woman—she was a pebble. If my life were a body of water, then she dropped into it and affected everything about me."

"Interesting."

"She affected my life like ripples in water."

"But to do so she had to have an impact in your life."

"She did. That's how the ripples came about, naturally. But for her to do so, she had to sink. She sank deep into my heart. The crevices of my heart. But it's hard to find a particular pebble in a body of water. So she's still there, in my heart, but there's nothing I can do about it. All I can do is watch the ripples continue to spread outward."

"What an image," Augustine remarked. "You are definitely a writer. But I like that. I guess we all have pebbles in our lives."

"I believe that to be true."

Augustine did not wish to press Henry more on his pebble. "So tell me about some of your books. Which one is your favorite?" Augustine asked, lightening the mood.

"Oh, I don't know about that. *Colorblind* was my first bestseller. I think that'll always have a place in my heart."

"Colorblind?" Augustine asked.

"That's the title of the book. It's about when love fails. Or, more correctly, when people fail in love. But most of my readers come out of it thinking love fails."

"I can see that," Augustine nodded. "Love doesn't fail; the people with the love do."

"Exactly. But maybe putting the blame on this abstract, faceless feeling that we call love makes it easier for people. Takes away the responsibility of failing."

"And do you address that in the book?" asked Augustine.

"No. And I think that's why people come out of it thinking love fails. So in my next book I'm going to explore similar themes, but more thoroughly and evolved."

"Good on you. Where can I buy *Colorblind?*"

Henry was about to name off three or four generic websites where it could be purchased, but then he remembered the copy in his bag.

"I have a copy in my bag. You can have it," Henry said, and reached for his bag.

"I don't want to take your copy."

Henry laughed. "It's my book. You can't take that from me. It's totally fine." He handed Augustine the book.

Augustine held the book with one hand and ran his other hand across the front of the hard cover. The copy itself seemed slightly aged, yet the mostly-white design was clean and nearly blemish-free.

"It has a beautiful cover," Augustine said sincerely.

"People say it's a beautiful book."

"What do you say?" Augustine looked at Henry as he said this.

"I say I put a great deal of myself in this book."

"Ah. A modern-day Hemingway," Augustine laughed.

"I wish," Henry replied, slightly blushing. He wanted to change the subject. "What did you do for a living, Augustine?"

He touched his mustache. "Boring office work that afforded me the comfort of buying pretty ladies flowers whenever they gave me attention. And now, in my retirement, allows me to travel."

"That sounds pretty nice." Henry leaned to his left and rested his head on his hand.

"Living off written words sounds even more nice," Augustine remarked.

"I suppose you're right." Henry stared off into the lobby. He thought about jellyfish. He looked to his left and out the window. He imagined the window as a looking glass into his heart. A jellyfish swam around and around, and its tentacles brushed where they pleased, and some even found their ways into veins. Henry sat up.

"Their tentacles spread," Henry whispered.

"What?" asked Augustine, slightly surprised by his whisper.

"The jellyfish—their tentacles spread out from our hearts. Hell, they even wrap around our brains. Loneliness affects our entire existence."

Augustine smiled in understanding. "That's when loneliness turns into depression."

"I see." Henry continued to stare out the window.

Augustine checked his watch and straightened up a bit. "They're going to call for us to board soon."

"Thank you for this conversation, Augustine. You've given me inspiration. You've given me some solace as well."

"I just didn't want either of us to be alone." As Augustine spoke, a lady came on over the intercom and called for first-class passengers to line up at the gate.

"Well, that's me," Augustine said. "I assume a published author such as yourself is flying first-class as well?"

"No, I'm coach," Henry replied, turning away from the window. "First-class is overrated."

"That may be true, but it's still comfortable. It was a pleasure meeting you, Henry. I look forward to reading about jellyfish, love, and Paris."

Henry smiled and stood up. He reached out his hand and shook Augustine's. "It was absolutely a pleasure."

Augustine grabbed his two bags and headed toward the gate. Henry sat down and looked at Augustine's back for a moment. He quietly thanked Augustine for his company, and then returned to looking out the window. He thought more about jellyfish, and how he will soon come across countless people surrounding the Eiffel Tower that will have jellyfish swimming in their hearts.

Chemicals

You walk into the kitchen and pull a pot out from under the stove. You lift the black, medium-sized pot to eye level, and, using the handle for obvious reasons, you twirl the pot a couple times to check and see if there are any remnants of food from previous uses. You performed this task two nights ago after pulling the same pot out of the steaming dishwasher, so this is more so double checking to make sure it is spotless.

You have always been this way: from making sure the cooks did not let your food touch while in college to only being able to sleep with your pillow at a certain angle, you had a particular way about certain things. Not everything, of course, but some things. As it is with most people, you found passion in some things, disgust in some things, and curiosity in some things. You always strove, and still strive, to work your way toward replacing curiosity with understanding, so perhaps the double checking (and sometimes triple checking) of your medium-sized pot is one of the many ways in which you obtain that understanding.

After turning the stove knob so that a neat, round flame comes into existence, or rather ignition, and placing the spotless pot on said flame, you turn and walk to your left and toward the sink to measure out six cups of water.

Look at you: married, two kids, a career you enjoy, a nice social life even at forty-one, and still you have the time and the desire to cook for your family each night (except for the nights you all go out as a family to eat, naturally). All of this, however, would be meaningless without happiness in your life. But you have that too, and so you count yourself blessed to have the life that you do. Not only did you marry your college sweetheart, but you still remain close to the friends that you called family while in college. You seldom think about college these days, although you have nothing but wonderful memories of the four years, because you live pleasantly in the present.

"Heather, come here, please," You shout upward, and a moment later you hear a door open from upstairs.

Heather, your seventeen-year-old daughter, calls from the top of the stairs: "What do you need, Mom?"

"I said to come here, so I think I need you to come here," you shout, and laugh a little, but quiet enough so that Heather does not hear.

You hear a faint sigh from the stairs, and then the pressing of feet against wooden planks. Heather, in a deep red and airy-white sun dress, appears in the kitchen entrance.

"Yes, Mom?" Heather asks, crossing her arms.

"Where's your boyfriend?" you say.

"Phil's still upstairs."

"On your bed?"

"Mom," Heather rolls her eyes.

You shout past your daughter: "Philip! Come down here please."

"Mom!"

"What? I need his help too."

"Oh my God." Heather walks over to the kitchen island and sits down on a barstool. You look at the stove and notice the pot is now boiling. You grab two bags of noodles and open each one.

"Yes ma'am?" Philip asks as he walks into the kitchen.

After dumping the noodles into the boiling water, you turn and face Philip.

"I need help," you say. "I need Heather to cut some tomatoes and set the table, and I figured you could keep her company. Maybe even cut some things too." You smile at Philip. He smiles back, albeit awkwardly.

"Sure. Whatever you need."

Heather gets up from the barstool and pinches Philip's side as she walks behind him to the cabinets. This reminds you of the countless times your thumb and index fingers have squeezed the obliques of your husband.

"Isn't Dad coming home tonight?" Heather asks, unknowingly speaking of the devil, as she pulls a few plates from the gray cabinet.

"He sure is. I've missed that man. Two weeks is too long," you reply.

"You've been married for, like, sixteen years. I'd say that that's too long," Heather says sarcastically.

Philip, awkwardly standing by the refrigerator, feels uneasy about Heather's comment on your marriage. You look at him and notice discomfort in his face.

"Eighteen years in two months, actually. And the moments I have spent with him have been beautiful." You say this in the hopes of putting Phil as ease and enlightening your daughter.

"Gross. Besides, we read an article in class a few days ago that talked about how love is ephemeral," Heather replies, butchering the pronunciation of "ephemeral."

"So is human life," you say. "But here I am: still alive and still in love."

"Human life isn't short," she says defiantly. "Ninety or a hundred years is a long time."

"Say that to a redwood," you say, and laugh. You turn back to the pot and stir the noodles so that they will unstick from the bottom of the pot. You hear a phone vibrate.

"Jazz just texted me. He said he won't be home for dinner," Heather says, staring down at her phone.

You turn around and face Heather. "Tell him there will be leftovers in the fridge." Heather puts her phone on the kitchen island and returns to setting the table. Philip walks over to the sink and washes his hands with the notion that he will be cutting the tomatoes. As you place a pan on the stove, you hear the front door open.

"I'm home," you hear your husband shout. The front door closes, and you hear him take off his shoes.

"We're in the kitchen, Dad," Heather replies as she sets down the last fork. You have been with your husband for twenty-three years, and married for almost eighteen, yet the thought of seeing him still gives you butterflies. You can feel the critters flap their wings as you stir the sauce in the pan. You hear him enter the kitchen, so you turn around.

"Victor, you're home," you exclaim, a mile-long smile stretching across your face. Victor sees this, and matches your smile.

"That's right," he replies, and walks over to you. He grabs you and kisses you. Lightly at first, but then another kiss that is more deep, more true to his longing for you over the past two weeks. Heather tugs on Philip's shirt in the background, and they leave. Victor pulls away from you slightly and stares at you. You're worried that he has noticed a new line forming on either side of your eyes—more talons for the crow's feet.

"Stop looking at my crow's feet," you tease.

"Why? When we were younger, your skin formed those lines whenever you laughed or smiled. Now it just looks like your eyes are always laughing. Always happy," Victor says with nothing but sincerity in his soft voice; the same voice that he used to use when putting the kids to sleep when they were actually kids, and not the teenagers that they are now.

"I am happy."

"How so?"

You want to make him feel important. "Because my mouth used to smile. Now my soul does."

"Your soul? How do you figure that?" he asks.

"The eyes are the windows to the soul, silly. If my eyes are always smiling—always happy—then that really only means my soul is."

Victor pulls you closer to him and wraps his arms around you. He digs his left hand into your hair, and you can feel the metal of his wedding ring touch your scalp. And you're happy to be back in his arms, with your cheek pressed against his chest, and your eyelids holding onto each other like the reunited hands of distant lovers. Your arms are squeezing his abdomen, allowing him minimal air, but all is fine because you are his breath.

The water from the pot begins boiling over, and this brings you back to reality. You let go of Victor and return to the food. You hear him take a breath. He wraps himself behind you and kisses your head.

"I love you," he says.

"I love you too," you reply, naturally.

"Where's Jazz?"

"He won't be home for dinner."

"Okay," he says, loosening his wrapped arms.

"His appointment is tomorrow."

"I know." Victor lets go of you. "I'm going to go take a quick shower before dinner."

"Hurry up," you reply. "It'll be ready soon."

"I've missed you," he says as he exits the kitchen. You stir the pasta in the pot, and the butterflies in your stomach continue to stir.

◆　◆　◆

It is 1:22am when Jazz quietly opens the front door. You, being upstairs and asleep, hear nothing. The creaking of the aged door irritates him as he tries to shut it slowly, so he grips the doorknob more firmly. Perhaps the tightness of his grip will transfer his frustration over to the door, and, somehow, in some way, will cause it to stop creaking. But that does not work.

"Shit," Jazz mutters, and clenches his jaw. The door finally reaches the frame. Jazz turns the knob, slides the door into place, and quietly latches the door. Jazz, your fifteen-year-old son, has dealt with certain issues for most of his life. Most of these you know about—his anger issues, his disregard for authority, and his soon-to-be diagnosed bipolar disorder—but there are some issues that you do not know about—the bullying he was subjected to while growing up, his moderate drug use, and his dream of being an airline pilot.

Jazz hates his name. Part of it has to do with being bullied as a child, as a lot of the kids picked on him for his name. Another part of it has to do with the fact that he hates jazz music, even though neither you nor Victor typically listen to jazz, and it did not really play a role in choosing the name for your son. Either way, Jazz, for some unknown, and consensually incorrect statement, believes that Miles Davis was a quack.

Life is not great for Jazz, and you know that. He often has episodes of anger, episodes of depression, and, other times, episodes of indifference—numbness, if you will. It is seldom that you see your son happy or enthusiastic about something. He has been seeing a psychiatrist, and the psychiatrist called the previous day and told you that she had a good idea of what may be going on in Jazz's head; she just wants one more session with Jazz to be sure. You understand that the brain is full of chemicals, and those chemicals can do sad and scary and bad things to people, but it is still hard. You wish you could do more for Jazz. You wish a lot of things, but above all, you wish happiness and stability for Jazz.

Being only fifteen-years old, Jazz knows that it is not acceptable to be out past a certain time—namely, past his ten o'clock curfew. But, being only fifteen, he does not necessarily care for or think about the rules that have been imposed upon him by you and his father. He decided months ago that he does well enough in school, so it should not really matter if he misses class, or smokes weed, or mouths off to the principal. Jazz is very intelligent—you know this; Victor knows this; and his teachers and administration know this. But Jazz has issues, and he internally struggles with these issues constantly.

"What were you doing out so late?" Heather asks in a whispered snap. Jazz is startled, and turns around to see Heather standing at the bottom of the stairs.

"I didn't hear the stairs crackle," Jazz responds.

"Well I heard the door. Where were you?"

"I was out with friends." Jazz begins walking away. Heather knows that Jazz does not really have any "friends," but rather people he gets into trouble with.

"What were you doing?" asks Heather.

"It doesn't matter," Jazz says, still walking away. "Go back to texting Philip or whatever."

Heather rolls her eyes and then turns to ascend the stairs. "You're lucky Mom or Dad didn't wake up."

"I don't give a shit," Jazz whispers loudly from the kitchen. The quiet of the house allows Heather to hear him. She sighs, closes her eyes for a few seconds, and then goes back to her room.

◆ ◆ ◆

"How are you feeling today?" the psychiatrist asks your son. Earlier, when she opened her office door to invite Jazz in, you saw her wearing a salmon-colored business skirt and blazer. Since salmon is your favorite color, this helped you feel a little at ease. *Maybe she did it on purpose. Did I ever tell her my favorite color?* you think as you sit in the waiting area.

"I feel all right. A little tired," Jazz responds instinctually. He keeps his eyes focused on his splitting shoelaces.

"Why do you feel a little tired?"

"Because life happens during the day *and* the night, yet we're expected to sleep during the night. I want to see what the night has to offer." Jazz chuckles quietly at his bullshit reply.

You check your watch and realize they have been in there for twenty minutes over the scheduled timeframe. You begin to worry. You pull out your phone and call Grace.

"Hello?" you hear after three rings.

"Grace! I have a question."

"What's going on, Amy? Is everything okay?"

"Yes. I was just wondering about counselor or therapy or what-have-you sessions. Is it normal for them to go over time? Jazz has had several sessions, and they have never gone over the hour, but this one has. Is that normal?"

"Of course that's normal. They must be having a good conversation. If the therapist—or whoever—isn't running out screaming, then everything is fine," Grace says, and giggles. You picture her covering her mouth with her other hand as she giggles. *O, Grace: so full of grace* you used to say to her in regards to her demeanor and composure.

"Thank you," you say, relieved. Grace says she has to go, and so you wish her well, and mention the need to meet up for brunch. She agrees and the phone call ends. Plans for brunch or girls' nights or coffee get-togethers have been mentioned for the past ten years, but they seldom come into fruition. You are busy with life, and she is undoubtedly busy with life, and you understand this, and you are sure she understands this, so there tends to be nothing but amicable conversations through the generation of radio waves from cellphone towers.

Silence lines itself around the frame of the waiting area; it reminds you of the nights you would find yourself in your dorm room during midterms and finals, and how quiet the entire floor would be. You have not thought about college in some time now, and this brings back a flood of nostalgia. The place where you met Victor; the place where you lost almost all your confidence at one point; the place where you persevered and excelled in the end; the place where you found yourself.

You grab the cliché heart necklace around your neck and fiddle with it, swinging it from side to side, as if you were touching your own heart, which is currently filled with nostalgia. Nostalgia feels the way it does because it is not a standalone emotion, but rather it is a mixture of emotions, a mixture of chemicals that reside in your brain. The chemicals currently making you feel happy yet melancholic are the same chemicals that keep your son awake at night and overwhelmingly sad.

Jazz emerges from the hallway that ended with the psychiatrist's office door. He sees you sitting in a black chair that is indistinguishable from all the others in the area, and he wonders why you chose to sit so far from the hallway. For a moment he considers that you wanted to respect his privacy and not listen in, but then he remembers how thick the lady's doors to her office are, and he concludes that the reason for your seating is irrelevant.

"Mom," Jazz says, and you snap out of your thoughts.

"Oh! Are you all done?" you ask. You look at the psychiatrist behind Jazz.

"Can I please have a quick word with you?" The psychiatrist asks.

"Of course." You grab your purse off the ground and follow the lady to her office. Jazz sits in one the black chairs and resumes staring at his shoelaces.

◆ ◆ ◆

"Victor," you say, lying in bed next to him. He is reading *The Park Bench Near the Eiffel Tower*, a novel recently published by your and Victor's college friend. You watch Victor's eyes run across the book's cream-colored page, his reading glasses lightly situated on his nose. Victor has aged wonderfully, but the years can be seen in his eyes: a light mist has made home in them, and the deep brown of his eyes has begun to fade like black coffee as the ice begins to melt. It is subtle, and you are probably the only person in existence who has noticed this fading beside Victor himself.

He puts his finger in between the pages and looks at you. "Yes?" he asks.

"Jazz was diagnosed today."

Victor is taken aback. His lower jar hangs down for a moment before speaking: "Why didn't you say something earlier?"

"Because the kids were around. Jazz obviously knows, but I don't want Heather to know yet."

"So what is it?" Victor asks while rubbing his forehead.

"He's bipolar and has depression. Something about anxiety, too."

Victor takes his finger out of the book. He removes his reading glasses and covers his face with his hands.

"The psychiatrist prescribed us medicine," you say.

"Oh my God." You hear Victor sniffle. He repeats himself two more times, rubbing his face slowly.

"It'll be okay," you say, almost pleadingly. You can feel your eyes swelling. It'll be okay."

Victor composes himself by sitting up and rubbing his eyes.

You let a few tears roll down your cheeks as you watch him. One tear finds itself in a wrinkle off-shooting from your upper lip. You wipe it away.

"It'll be okay," Victor says, half to you, and half to himself. He nods. You stare at him. He looks blurry through your watery eyes. Victor nods and looks at you. "It'll be okay," he says again, this time looking directly into your eyes, a slight smile budding on his face. The scruff on his face moves with the receding of his cheeks.

You stare at him. "You need to shave," you say, wiping a tear away with your wrist.

"I always shave in the morning," he replies.

"I know."

He smiles and kisses you. Pressing his lips against yours, the salty flavor your tears left behind seeps into your mouth. You are sure Victor can taste it, but you are also sure that he doesn't mind.

"Go back to reading. Everything will be okay," you say, and reach for your pen and notebook from the nightstand.

Victor's eyes linger on you as he adjusts his glasses. He watches you begin to write your nightly entry—whatever is it that you write, as Victor has no clue. You scribble and take breaks. When not writing, you hold your pen as close to your mouth as lovers and matching socks ought to be to each other. You hold your pen between your fingers loosely—carelessly—yet perfectly. It twirls airily as you think of the next word to write down. Your pen glides across your paper, leaving a trail of black gold in the form of loops and tails and periods. It swims between the strands of your hair as you reread your honeyed sentences.

"You are so beautiful," Victor says finally. You look up at him and blush. Even after all these years he still makes you blush.

"Stop!" you say, and bite your tongue as you smile.

You kiss him.

◆　◆　◆

Weeks pass, and bottles of pills are consumed. Jazz goes through several stages of emotions. You worry the medication is doing more harm than good. Eventually, though, his mood stagnates.

"How are you today, Jazz?" you ask. The two of you are sitting alone in the kitchen. He is snacking on some chips, and you are sipping on some black tea.

"I feel fine. How are you, Mom?"

"I'm doing well." You take a sip.

"That's good. Oh, I got an A on my oral presentation in English."

That's great!" you exclaim, and smile. Jazz smiles too, but hides it.

"When is Dad coming home?"

"In three days," you say, and stare at Jazz. He is staring at the bag of chips. You feel his heart. You feel relieved that he is doing better, but you worry about his future. Will he spend the rest of his life on medication in order to feel remotely "normal"? Your eyes swell. You take another sip.

"I love you, Jazz."

Jazz looks up at you. "I love you too, Mom."

Grace

Age 0

Grace is born, and her parents become infinitely happier. Their hearts grow much like the Grinch's heart did.

Grace cries just as much as babies tend to, and this keeps her parents close by. This should keep all parents close by.

Age 3

Grace wears pigtails almost everyday. Her mother wishes she would change it up, but she does not. This goes on for a year.

Grace's father is awarded "Teacher of the Year." He celebrates by buying the family a new SUV.

Grace, through perseverance only a three-year old could posses, learns how to swim. She is terrified of the "sharks in the deep end," and refuses to swim on that side of any pool. She lets it be known one day that "Dad is not enough to save me" from the sharks, and so she does not swim with him on that end.

Age 7

Grace and Amy meet. They swap shoes and become inseparable friends.

Grace's parents, after trying unsuccessfully for four years, decide to put to rest the idea of another child. They decide that Grace is, and always has been, enough.

Grace decides one morning in May that ladybugs are her favorite bug. She vows to love all ladybugs as much as "the moon and sun love each other." Or, at least, as much as they should love each other.

Grace begins habitually biting her nails.

Age 12

Grace is graced with a "gift" from Mother Nature: menarche. Her mom has a long conversation with her that evening while her dad watches a show in the living room with knots tightening in his stomach.

Grace finds love in strawberry smoothies. She gets one every Sunday with her dad, and he gets a banana smoothie every Sunday with Grace.

Grace begins a sunglasses collection. From blue to black to brown to gray, she wants them all.

Grace goes to a girls camp in the summer. Amy does not go, and this saddens both of them. She has a great time, but misses home and Amy the entire time.

Grace wants a pet rat for Christmas. Santa gives Grace a rat for Christmas. She names him Albert.

Age 16

Grace gets her license, and a car. She cries at the sight of it. "More than I deserve," she says in the driveway, standing next to the deep-red car. Her parents smile and tell her that she is more than they deserve. They all cry together.

Grace and Amy go on a road trip in the summer. They meet cute boys and swim in warm waters. Amy talks each night on the trip about how she did not think Grace's parents would let Grace go on the trip. Each night, Grace agrees.

Grace, after years of watching her parents, decides she wants to become a marriage counselor so that she can help all couples be like her parents. She looks into colleges.

Grace gets asked out on dates a record amount of times this year. She goes on three of the fourteen dates proposed to her. One boy makes it to a fourth date, but he realizes she was "too much of a prude" and breaks it off. She is okay with this.

Grace talks on the phone with Amy almost every night. Amy primarily talks about gossip around school, and Grace primarily listens. Like all friends, they have their arguments, but they all end—unlike their friendship.

Grace realizes that sun dresses are absolutely the best type of clothing to ever exist, and so she buys a quarter of her closet worth. She wears several of them on the road trip, and receives plenty of compliments.

Age 18

Grace applies to several universities. She gets accepted to all but one of them. She decides to go to CSU Long Beach. Her father graduated from there, and he found her mom (as well as himself) there, so she finds it to be a beautiful thing to go there as well.

Grace convinces Amy to apply to the same school. She gets accepted as well. They celebrate by staying up all night and watching *Sixteen Candles*.

Graces goes to Santa Monica to meet Amy and a few other friends on the pier. She orders a strawberry smoothie, and some boy around her age grabs her smoothie by mistake. He gives it back to her and she leaves.

Grace graduates high school. She cries as she hugs bodies that she spent four years with, but will probably never see again. She thinks about how it was a smart move to wear waterproof mascara.

Grace spend the summer reading books and working. Amy often comes into her work to bug her. Grace does not mind this; she enjoys Amy's company more than cats enjoy their chins being scratched.

Grace and Amy get the same dorm room. They move in together at the end of the summer. They meet two sophomore guys.

Grace, almost nineteen, breaks the heart of a good man. This process breaks her heart as well. As time goes on, they remain friends, but awkwardness fills the silence in their conversations.

Age 21

Grace loses her virginity. She does not regret this, but she wishes she would have been in love rather than in lust. She vows to be in love the next time.

Grace realizes that one day she and Amy will not be as close as they are now. This causes her to cry on four separate occasions. Grace bites her nails an excessive amount during this time.

Grace gets drunk for the first time. She enjoys it at first, but then she doesn't. She drinks only on occasion after this.

Grace misses her parents. She decides to visit them most weekends. Amy sometimes goes with her, but most of her weekends are spent with Victor instead.

Grace spends two hours lying in the grass with ladybugs one afternoon outside one of the classroom buildings. She reminisces about her childhood, and becomes overly nostalgic. She misses her childhood innocence, but knows she must continue to grow.

Grace puts away her childish things and focuses on her schooling and progression toward her future career. Amy, with the help of Grace and Victor, eventually does the same.

Age 26

Grace starts her career as a marriage counselor. It is tough, and she often times feels less experienced than others due to the fact that she is not married. She loses sleep over this.

Grace tries to be a vegetarian. It lasts for two weeks.

Grace moves an hour away from Amy (and Victor), but the distance feels much greater. She tears up almost every time they talk on the phone, which becomes a weekly occurrence rather than a daily one.

Grace finds out that Amy is pregnant with her second baby. She cries the whole car ride over, and then cries while hugging Amy. Heather greets Grace by calling her "Aunt Gracie."

Grace, feeling lonely in her apartment, buys a small dog. Henry always sends his short stories to her, and in them he frequently talks about dogs. She wonders if this influenced her.

Age 30

Grace falls in love. He is tall; he is kind; and he is emotionally available. they are together for four months before she tells him that she loves him, although she had felt it after only two months. He says, "I love you too" a month later.

Grace has more clients than she ever has. She works endlessly. She loves it.

Grace takes her boyfriend to her favorite smoothie shop in Los Angeles. She, of course, orders a strawberry smoothie; he orders a banana smoothie. It is a Sunday, and this all reminds her of her father. She calls him.

Grace buys a small house. She decides she will live and work in her current location indefinitely. Love, marriage, and family are on her mind.

Age 35

Grace's father passes away. She is heartbroken: partly because she misses him, and partly because she does not wish for her mother to live without him. She cries herself to sleep fifteen times in two months.

Grace gets engaged. He moves into her small house. It is now their small house. She sleeps better at night.

Grace reads *The Sun Also Rises* for the first time and finds new vigor in life. She thanks Hemingway at random times throughout the year.

Age 41

Grace's mother passes away. She buries her next to her father, and prays for them. They are together again, in a way.

Grace realizes that she will probably never have kids of her own. She and her husband adopt a baby. Their small house becomes even smaller, but even more full of love and family.

Age 44

Grace takes her child to get a smoothie. Grace orders a strawberry smoothie, and, as she has done several times throughout her life, she thinks about the boy who grabbed her smoothie in Santa Monica when she was just a teenager. She wonders what he is doing in life at this moment, at this age. She closes her eyes. She wishes, with all her heart, that that boy is happy, and that he is doing fine. She takes a drink of her smoothie and walks on, holding her child's hand.

Part II

Poetry and Prose

Some of this is good; some of this is not so good.

Dedicated to all the people in my life that make me feel. Thank you for the emotional memories.

And thank you to Charles and Cristian. You have been with me through it all.

I'm just a miner looking for gold,
But the walls are caving in,
Crushing my heart and my soul.

I'm sitting here,
And I'm starting to think.
And I'm growing concerned
That you never actually cared.
I'm worried; I'm second-guessing;
I'm scared.
Because you've told me that you do,
But those are just words in the end.
And your actions have betrayed your sentences
Time and time again.
Should I continue only listening to you?
Or should I listen to my family and friends?
And it's not that they're against us;
They're against you.
Because they claim that you're rotten,
And if I stay with you,
I'll become rotten too.
I'm starting to believe them—
That because of you I've changed,
Because I've noticed how I think about things now
And how my smile isn't the same.
Maybe they're right;
Maybe you're not good for me.
It's as if, because of you,
I'm slowly dying;
I've forgotten how to breathe.
Or maybe you're just suffocating me.
But either way,

I think I need to come up for some air.
And when I get to the surface,
I don't think you should be there.
I ended up on the path with the most footprints,
And you're all I got.
Perhaps it's time for me to turn around,
And give the other trail a shot.

-Relearning How to Breathe

I see now what people mean
When they say they see God in nature.
It was unexpected,
Serendipitous,
I had put in no wager.
This finding was sincere.

I was standing there,
On the pier,
And I saw the sun in the West
And I saw her, standing there,
In a white-blue dress.
There was a breeze
Sweeping over the ocean's waves,
And that paced air
Caused its own little ocean in her hair.
Her hair danced with and against the breeze,
And in that moment I forgot how to breathe.

She turned against the sun,
Toward me,
And only certain features I could see.
I saw her Da Vinci freckles,
And her omnibenevolent smile.
She saw right through my person,
And continued gazing for a while.
And my heart pined for her.

She was the personification of nature,
Chloris herself.

And through her I saw God.
But I wished not to devote myself
To the trees, the mountains, or the birds.
I wished only to devote myself to her.
She made my soul agog.

She was ten feet away,
But the moon seemed closer.
Carpe Diem, right?
I had to seize the day.
I had to seize her, my new light.
The sun went down,
As the earth spun us around,
And I followed her, chalantly,
Through the town.

I'll never forget when she turned,
And looked at me with those hazel-brown eyes
And with that perfect smile,
She said, "Hi."
The world was all right.
I was all right.
She was perfect.
And that was the night
I fell in love.

   -Love at First Sight
      ("Chalantly" is not a word)

I have memorized the rhythm of your heart in all its different variations, whether that be excitement, happiness, or, regrettably, even sadness. I have slept on your chest more times than I have slept on my own pillow, and your bosom has comforted me more than any amount of cotton or silk ever could. The ebb and flow of your blood coming in and out of your ventricles is as soothing to me as the rain coming down outside my window. The raindrops of your heart are the last things I hear at night and the first things I hear in the morning. I long to end my days listening to the beat, beat, beat of your chest as you trace the freckles on my arm with your finger and with the gentle care I once thought only possible from a mother. I only wish one day I end my selfishness so that you may memorize the drumming of my heart, and then we can work on living—and loving—in the same tempo.

-The Raindrops of Your Heart

I know. I'm forty-five years old and I have a newborn baby. Believe me; I'm a woman of science, and I know. But he's a healthy baby, and I had a healthy birth. But, looking at him, I do admit that it makes me sad. It makes me sad that, statistically speaking, I will die before he will. I will potentially miss out of some major events in his life. If I live to be eighty-five, he will only be forty. He will live half his life without me. If not more. And that makes me sad because, if everything goes perfect in this world, then I will never live without him. But that means that he will live without me. So how is that perfect? I know he will have a significant other by then, and kids by then, but I am still his mother. I was the one who supplied him with the 100,000 calories while inside of me, and I will be the one to give him millions more. I will have been the one who will wake up countless times throughout the years just to put him back to sleep. I will have been the one to dress him, bathe him, take him to school, and love him with all that I am. But the paradoxical aspect about this whole parenting thing is that I want to do it more than anything I have ever done. How could I not love something that came from my very womb? He will always be a part of me.

-Motherhood

I'm a good person. I've never broken someone's heart without breaking my own heart in the process.

I ask not for forgiveness,
Or redemption.
I don't need exemption
From my doings unrighteous.
All I desire is that blanket of dirt.
Six feet deep,
Where I can have that eternal sleep.
Death, what a wondrous flirt.

You look at all the lights that make up this place,
And you say,
"We're just dust aimlessly floating through space."
And you feel out of place.
But then along comes a girl,
And she captivates your being,
So you decide to make her your world.
And in a great, big, cosmic rush
You fall in love.
And you say,
"I love you."
And with a blush
She says, I love you too."
So with this love,
You look in a different direction:
You look above.
You gaze at the specks of light
That seem to give guidance in the night,
And you think about that girl
Who has become your world.
And everything is all right.
You're not just floating through space;
You're that girl's soulmate—
That girl's guiding light,
And you feel right in place.

-A Change

"Is there anyone out there?" the old man implored.
"No," replied the Universe, laughing.

I haven't been sleeping well lately. I lie in bed for several hours with my eyes closed, but sleep doesn't come to me. It's similar to how I walk around all day with a smile on my face, but happiness has yet to come to me.

The way the feelings simmer and then fall,
Such as when my heart would throb when she'd call,
But then apathy encroaches,
And indifference is "felt" as she approaches.

I know not the changing's reason;
Perhaps it's the change in season.
Or I just grow lazy and tired;
And so it goes: every slacker eventually gets fired.

But I swear that I did love her.
But then again, I'm not so sure.
Maybe I just don't possess the right mix of chemicals.
Maybe love is smooth, and I'm nothing but wrinkles.

Wrap the curtains over the breathing window,
And light a candle;
Watch the flame mimic the dancing curtains,
And watch me move my hand to your cheek;
Feel my fingers trace your hairline,
And feel the temperature in your face rise;
Exhibit atomic repulsion by moving closer to me,
And feel your breath grow harder than the window's.

The birds have finished their songs,
But ours has just begun;
You move closer.
What's the difference between love and lust?
I know I'd be content stopping now and holding you instead,
So perhaps that's the difference.
I love every atom that comprises your being —
Even if I can only see the result and not the individual pieces;
And that's because it's all you:
Your chemicals,
Your electric currents,
Your heartbeat,
Your freckles,
And even your vocal cords
Are the result of the stars burning up
Just to fuel the creation that is you;
And I am confounded.

Feel your clothes slip off your shaking body
As my hands lead their descent to the floor;
Feel my middle finger trace your collarbone,
And hear me laugh when you tremble as I approach your breasts;
Close your eyes as my face draws near,
And wrap your tongue around mine.
Wrap your existence around mine.

-Dying Stars/Living Universe

I don't like ending the day. Calling it a day means I will be going home, and that means I will be going home to not you. And, since I am in a state of mind where all I want is you, that does not go well. So I will sit on my couch and think, once more, how I screwed up, and how I lost you, and how I lost everything that mattered to me. I don't understand how the days are bearable, yet the nights (or rather, the darkness and the silence) drive me mad. You're out in the world living. Well, you were my world. So where am I supposed to live now?

The concept of maturity is alien to nostalgia. My brain is wrapped with gauze that has been marinated in years of experiences, short-comings, and once-in-a-lifetime moments. But when the scent of rain on a cloudy day hits my nostrils, I am transported back to that little kid sitting in the elementary classroom, staring out the window and feeling infinitely close to my classmates. With the gray of the sky seeping into the classroom, and the chilly air being fought off by the building's heater, we all share missing-teeth smiles and cuddled pantomimes in our sweaters. Perhaps nostalgia (much like diesel is to gasoline) is the byproduct of a memory. Nostalgia is the chemical equivalent of a time machine.

"If you don't care, and I don't give a shit,
Then the ceiling fan will never get hit,"
You said, slowly taking off your pink shirt;
I smiled, knowing one of us would get hurt.

Your legs, bent and erected like mountains;
The passion comes in tons, not in ounces.
I took my time, as if picking flowers,
And my head your mountains did embower.
And, in the valley, a cave of damp warmth
Beckoning me to travel steadfast North,
Yet you didn't want all of me in there,
Only for the physical did you care;
But you whispered sweet lies into my ear,
Causing me to feel, to feel like Shakespeare.

I'd "tame the ardent beast," as you would say.
And I'd go home after a sex-filled day,
Knowing this was the worst time of my life—
But you enjoyed this, so it was all right.
"You make me moan so loud," you would remark,
"That even heavenly angels would hark."

My body, my soul, and my heart are sore;
And I simply can't do this anymore.

Like rain, my tears revealed what was buried,
And you unearthed all the weight I carried.
And you were malcontent to say the least;
Underneath there was not some primal beast,
But rather a primal berry picker
(Watching my moment of greatness flicker)
Wishing to pluck your heart out of your chest,
And, in my warm hands, have it safely kept.

But my feelings are not what you wanted,
So all that I had for you was stunted;
All of me—I would have given you all,
But you closed your arms, and you let me fall.

-Friends With Benefits

Garrett Willis

At the end of the day, and once I am settled in with the thoughts of my soul (the same thoughts which seem to keep me from sleeping most nights), I always come to the same conclusion about what I want from you, and what I want from us. I wish for our hearts no longer to be two separate systems, but instead two pieces reliant on the other in order to function. Perhaps your heart could be a boat, and mine could be a sail. Working together as one, my heart could guide yours, and your heart could give meaning to my existence, for without a sail a boat has no direction, and without a boat a sail has no meaning. I want my heart to be absolutely dependent upon yours. I want the blood that flows out of your heart to flow into mine. I want the same oxygen to be carried by the same blood. I want to meld into one with you.

The only thing that gets me up in the morning is the promise and certainty that one day I will not get up.

I died. Time has passed, and my body has decomposed completely. My thoughts and electrical currents have been lost to the void, but my atoms have gone elsewhere; they are swimming in the depths of the cosmos, and building the bark on trees; they are layering the mountains with snow, and rising as ash from the ruins of abandoned prospects.

I have died, and, thanks to the wonders of time, I have been forgotten by man, but I will be forever revered by the universe.

I have contributed more in death than I ever could have while living.

And now, look at you: you're the result of random chance and the dying of stars. And because of me, you are alive. Some of your atoms are my atoms—just merely recycled. You are inhaling the atoms that built the walls of my heart; the warmth that you feel in the pasture in which you lie is made possible by the sun burning up what was once me. I would say that I wish I could reach out from the void and touch you, but having bits of me wrapped around your soul seems to be enough.

-Death and Atoms and Stuff

After affectionate afterthoughts
I have come to conclude:
Roses in the summer afternoon
Are better off wilting
Than trying to compare to her.

Beauty is best when subtle—
Such as when the setting sun
Shines silently off the sea,
And how it reflects the same
Off her ocean of brunette.

Crashing water on the shores,
The waves are a mirror of her:
She is young, yet an old soul
Just as each wave is new,
Yet the contents are the age of the ocean itself.

Darkened rooms and lit candles
Are often a precursor to finding
Her fingers intertwined with mine,
And I'd much rather the sky break apart
Than have her fingers break from mine.

Even I would take the place of Atlas,
For I ask not for lighter burdens,
But for broader shoulders
So that I may bear the weight
Of the baggage that she brought with her.

Fighting and slaying a dragon to save her
Would be an easy and noble task
If I happened to own a sword—
And if I lived in the Middle Ages—
And if dragons existed.

Going about living the
Life of a salesman
(And all that it would entail)
Wouldn't be so bad
If she were my Linda.

Hell is not entirely hot when
Speaking of all its levels;
And she'd be worth the trip
To the ninth circle
If that were where she lie.

I am but a homely man
Who is in love with a woman
Who was thoughtfully forged
In the very heart of God Himself,
And has been living in mine ever since.

Jokes, laughs, and tears
Fill our days that are spent together:
Just as bees fill a hive;
It comes with a sense of wholeness,
And leaves behind a scent of something sweet.

Kings often long to love
A queen or woman or human
The way I love her,
But this love is pure,
And power is inevitably corrupt.

Let jesters poke fun
At the sticky sap
That encapsulates my words;
Only those who have never
Known love make it into a joke.

My cheeks become aflame when
Her touch makes impact,
And the butterflies take flight
When her smile reveals itself;
After all this time I still feel all of this.

And I wouldn't want it any other way.

- Scattered Thoughts on the Subject of Love

I have countless times found comfort in flirting with the notion of suicide.

When I first saw you on the sidewalk I hugged you because in that moment your existence exceeded my expectations. I was already interested in you from your pictures and words on a screen. But seeing you in real life broke all ceilings. It hasn't been long since we started talking, but feelings work outside of time. They say the world is my oyster, but what if I want you to be my shell? Will you wrap yourself around me, and make me feel safe? Will you let me try my best everyday to make you feel safe? If beauty is in the eye of the beholder, then so should perfection. I hold and acknowledge your beauty in one hand, and with the other hand I hold onto your perfection. In a little over three days you have filled up the emptiness that was inside me, and, because of you, I no longer feel alone. I've always been one to wear my heart on my sleeve, but you make it so that it doesn't feel vulnerable. You are extraordinary, ~~Jessica~~.

-A Text I Sent

They say there's plenty of fish in the sea,
But dammit -
She was the ocean to me.
Especially vivacious,
She made me sick with love.
And caused me to overflow with empathy.
But it's all gone now,
And so is she.

I hope that one day -
Oh please let it slip -
Let it slip one day.
I hope it slips off the tip of your tongue.
And between you two,
It fills the air.
And lingers there.
The slip of my name.
The past you tried -
So hard -
To hide.
It'll never be the same.

I thought it was all good,
But it turns out that I was the dragon,
And you were the damsel in dire
Need of help.
And so he came,
In his tested armor,

And slayed me.
Took you to safety,
While I drowned in the memories.

And so I was slain
But I was reborn,
Like a phoenix,
Into someone stronger.
Someone better
Someone right for you

So please,
Let it slip - my name
And nothing will ever be the same.
And he'll leave,
And you'll realize that
I'm still here,
Waiting for you.
Waiting for us.
That I am the one.

-Some Lame Song I Wrote Years Ago

I could not have guessed that it would all be a waste. All the letters I wrote; all the words I meticulously placed; everything I said—for nothing. I thought you to be a safe haven for the selective and meaningful words I bestowed onto you. But rather, you took them in like a dumping ground, and the words wilted in-between the folds of your neurons. Perhaps your electrical currents tore them apart, or the chemicals in your brain poisoned them. Either way, my words, or, I guess, my former words, have lost their meaning, even the three most sacred words I gave to you: "I love you."

-Wasted Words

I stopped at a red light, and I looked to my left and saw the passenger of the work truck next to me stick his hand out. His thumb was dancing to the beat of whatever was playing from that truck's speakers. But I knew that that hand was the hand of a man who just wanted to go home and see his family and hold his wife and kiss his kids on their heads and tell them all how much he loves them. But if he did that then he wouldn't be able to afford a living for his family; that's why he's pulling a double shift for the third night in a row. So why is he still calling it a double shift when he should call it a sextuple shift? He's being pulled from both ends: one end from his family, and the other end by his job and responsibilities. He's worried one will tear off his limb before the other, but he knows either way he would lose his family. That is why he is trying his best, and hoping the fruits of his labor are satisfactory. He hasn't tasted the fruits for himself, so he has no way of knowing whether they're sweet, or just rotten. But he does know that he's only been able to taste bitterness for a long time now. He just wants to go home to his family.

-The American Dream

I'm glad, without a doubt, that I got to experience what we had. I would not trade the feelings and emotions that were created inside of me for anything the world has to offer. But now it is all just memories. And to me, memories are useless. They do nothing but take up space in my mind, and there is no reason for me to keep these memories around, yet they are stuck in my cortex. And the sweet memories have become bitter, and now the emotions they invoke are sour and they make me choke. Yes, I believe it is better to have loved and lost than never to have loved at all. But I loved, and I lost. And I still love, and now I am lost.

I don't want to fall into this alone! I will have no one to hold on to on the way down, and I'll lose sense of direction. I don't want to hit the bottom alone. I don't want to look around for you only to find that you kept your distance from the edge, and I foolishly took the plunge. All this will do is drive us further apart, both emotionally and, consequently, physically. But as I say all this I can already feel myself losing balance, and there you are, taking a step back. So I fall. And fall. And shut my eyes and reach out for you, only to feel the air resistance between my fingers. It gets darker, and emotional turmoil takes root in my brain as I come into impact with the ground. I look around into vacancy. You're not here, and you never will be. You were never going to be. This is unrequited love.

I have this pit inside me—
This pit that's deep
And it's filled with emptiness.
How contradictory,
How paradoxical,
How shitty.

And I know I can't fill it—
This empty-filled pit—
With a view of the setting sun,
Or a gaze up at the lambent stars.
But I think—
I think—
I can fill it with the sound of you
Breathing next to me
At one in the morning.
With the darkened room
Still, and the porch light
Lightly seeping in through the window,
And the dim light gently touching
The wall.
Touching the wall the opposite way
Of how I touched it
When you said you were leaving.

I found myself drunk the other night—
Not that you'd be surprised;
I found myself thinking:

I thought of you;
I thought of me;
I thought of us.
And I realized that the fingers
That have intertwined with yours
Are the same ones that
Have slid across your cheeks in anger.
I'm not a perfect person; I know that.
I'm not a good person; I know that.
I'm an asshole; I know that.

I wish I could say you made me want to change,
But, in a way, you enabled me—
Not that it was your fault;
It was always my fault;
I know that now.
I saw you as a canvas
On which I could plant my paintbrushes.

I wish you the best.
You and I both know
That it wasn't me.
It never was,
And it never will be.

If, by some chance,
I left a minuscule pit in you,
I hope you're able to fill it

With a view of the setting sun,
Or a gaze up at the stars.

-Paradox

Grandpa, Grandpa, Grandpa:
Do you remember when you told me
You would take me for my first drink
Once I turned twenty-one?
"I'll show you a man's drink;
It'll cleanse your palette," you said.
Sixteen-year-old me waited,
Rejecting party offers from friends;
"I'm waiting for my grandpa
To take me out," I would say.

Grandpa, Grandpa:
Do you remember when you told me
That it was okay for me to try
A cigarette on my eighteenth birthday?
"I've been smoking for sixty years;
One or two drags won't hurt you," you said.
Seventeen-year-old me waited
With no real anticipation;
"I'll try it once;
I bet it's what a man would do," I would say.

Grandpa:
Do you remember when you told me
All these promises,
Or are you forgetting those too?
"Who are you?
Who is this lady next to me in these photos?" you said.

Twenty-year-old me cried
For you countless times;
"It's no one's fault—not yours or his;
It's the Alzheimer's," Mom would say.

For the first time in a long time you popped into my mind, and I'm not mad that you did. I'm just disappointed that it's fine that I no longer think about you. What once was a factor in every thought of my mind is now a part of my past. You are no longer a factor in the unfolding of my thoughts.

We are to the point where not only is the bridge burned, but I can't even recognize you on the other side of the canal. And it's sad that we went from making deep connections, and saying things we've never told anyone, to being strangers. It's unbelievable, and yet the clock ticks on, the page turns, and we take another breath.

It was the first time in a long time you popped into my mind, but it will be the last time. I said goodbye physically a long time ago, but I am now saying goodbye mentally.

I wrote so many words for you,
Which formed so many worlds,
And with one word—
You became Death,
The destroyer of them all.

The years—how they have passed us,
And how our bodies have changed;
I often find myself tracing the wrinkles
That have etched themselves into your face—
O, how each line is filled with such grace.
I love to waste the evenings tracing
The precipices of your crow's feet—
Of your micro canyons.
God constructed the Grand Canyon
Out of both earth and cellulose,
But I love your ravines the most.

I think love is letting your cat scratch you;
Love is letting your baby spit up on you—
Again and again and again;
Love is giving up bits of yourself for someone
And not thinking of it as a sacrifice
Or as compromise;
Love is opening your heart
Even though you know about the risks of infection
And possible destruction.

Whenever I smell paint I'm reminded of you. Well, reminded of us. Reminded of us painting our baby's room. Sorry, unborn baby. Forever unborn. Miscarriages will do that I suppose. But you know that. You know that better than I. I simply held you while you cried. Cried and bled. I felt a tinge of emptiness in me, sure, but I can't imagine how deep your pit must have been. Or still is. I don't know how the present is treating you; I just hope you're not still living in the past. Living in a time when the baby was supposed to. But I'm here—in the present. It's lonely without you, and a little cold. I wish you were here to fit your body around mine and warm me up. But who's to say I would be able to keep you warm? Wherever you are, maybe you're keeping our baby warm. I like to think that you are.

-Warmth

That isn't some angelic glow radiating from your soul; it's just the sun reflecting off the mixture of your makeup and forehead grease. So why don't you step down from your fantastic throne made of fantasies and delusions, and join all the peasants to whom you denied your affection. You're getting older, and yet you still believe some knight will come, as shiny as your face, to take you away. Sure, the ones who have asked for your hand are plebs in shitty garments, but their hearts were gold. And, frankly, your being is even shittier than their mixed fabrics. No one's going to slay a dragon for you because you've got nothing left to give after all the men came into your room to "slay" you. Are you a cat? How many lives do you have?

You can do your hair however you want, and you can wing your eyeliner whichever way you please, but your core will still be rotten, and now neither gold-plated men nor sewer rats want anything to do with you. You're nothing but a stray cat, and, if it were up to Iago, you would be drowned.

-An Angry Man's Ramblings

You're absolutely beautiful. I don't know if it's the way your eyes look, or the shape of your nose, but it touches a part of my brain that makes me think you're extraordinary beautiful. I can't get over it. I don't want to get over it.

-Early Draft of Something

Every phrase is just an expression
Until it's put into a practice.
I could tell you that I love you,
But let me always look at you with a half smile on my face;
Let me kiss you goodnight every night;
Let me get down on one knee and ask you a question;
Let me stand in front of you and answer a question with "I do;"
Let me dance with you;
Let me hold back your hair until the morning sickness passes;
Let me hold your hand as you bring our baby into this world;
Let me paint your favorite wall of our house with your favorite color;
Let me buy you flowers on your birthday, our anniversary, on
Valentine's Day, and on any day I feel you deserve them
(Let me buy you flowers every day);
Let me hold you with our child on our laps as we watch an ani-
mated movie about friendship;
Let me graze my thumb over your forming crow's feet and tell you
that you've never looked better
(And actually mean it);
Let me take you to your dream locations throughout our life
together, and after we retire;
Let me help you down the stairs on the days that your arthritis
hurts a little too much;
Let me fall asleep beside you on our bed of fifty some-odd years;
Let me be buried next to you;
Let me nourish the world with you;
Let me show you that I love you.

-In Practice

The brain operates off of electrical currents and chemicals. The electrical currents keep us thinking and alive, and the chemicals influence our thinking and if we want to be alive.

Let our blood pressure rise
With the ocean's tide.
We've sat here long enough
To know both our lives have been rough.
Shake the fine sand off your torso
And move a little closer.
Your hair smells nice,
And looks nice too.
All of you looks nice.
Thank you for choosing
To be here with me in this moment,
(Even if it's just for a moment).
If we go back to our normal lives tomorrow,
At least I'll know that,
For one brief moment,
You chose to live a sliver of your life
With me.
And that is more than I could have—
Or would have—
Ever asked.

-Drunken Words

You know when you're binge watching something on TV, and every now and then the screen goes to black as the scene changes, and then you see your reflection in the screen and feelings of discomfort and resentment touch your chest for a brief moment before the show lights up again?

Well, that's how I constantly feel. I am constantly staring at an image of myself that I do not wish to see, but the screen never lights up again. Just blackness. Just me looking at me.

She was the lights and movements and sounds that used to be plastered on the screen that is my life. But scenes change, and episodes end, and series get canceled. So does love. So did mine.

A spark
A spark is all that's needed
For an engine
     A stove
          A forest fire
               Love

The spark itself
Is not these things
Of course not
But the spark is what
Leads these things into
Their most excitable states

Los Angeles
With its
Rivers of metal
Channeling down
Various asphalt canals,
And its
Towers of glass
With ties and collars
Running and sitting inside,
This is home.

I'm still searching for remnants of you
In the rusty chambers of my heart,
But I've come across no residue;
Not even your scent plays a part
In the downtempo rhythm of my heart.

If winter is meant to break your heart,
Why does April exist in spring?

I was playing the piano for some twenty-year-old college student while my wife gave birth to our first child. While my wife cried and clenched her teeth in pain, I was seducing one of my former students in the poorly lit music building on campus. It wasn't the first time I cheated on my wife, and it wasn't the last, but I remember this one because, well, she was giving birth to my child at the time.

I was in a bar one time after work, and an older man began talking to me. We eventually got on the subject of adultery—without my bringing it up. He said something along the lines of: "If you decide to cheat on your wife, wait at least three years after you're married." I don't remember his reasoning, but I remember that I just smiled and nodded, as I had cheated on my wife even before she was my wife.

I have never felt
More pressure in my life
Than when I think
Of asking you to marry me.

More pressure is
Exerted onto my brain
Than the amount of pressure
It took to form
The diamond in my pocket.

Many people are inspired
By the changing of the season,
But it is the metamorphoses
That you have gone through
(And still wanted me through all)
That fill my pen with ink.

Nature and the ol' moon
Dictate that ocean waves
Crash against hills and rocks,
And, likewise, love and fate
Dictate that your hair's waves
Crash against my face
When you swoop in for a kiss.

I read once that all human breath is warm,
And, with your breath, I find this to be true;
But, recently, there has been a reform:
Distance has crept in-between me and you.
There is distance, and there is entropy,
So your breath can only travel so far
Before entropy saps the energy;
Your breath grows cold halfway from where you are.
I've tried so hard to feel your warmth again,
But to no avail; it's all so fruitless;
Finding your warmth must be something arcane,
And I'm just living a life that's bootless.
So I will lie in our old, frozen sheets,
And freeze in the presence of our defeats.

How should I convey to you how I feel,
But have it sound heightened, but still be real?
Call you beautiful? No, no, something new;
Perhaps I should write a poem about you.

I'm worried about semantic satiation;
I want to call you beautiful all the time,
But I don't want the word to lose meaning—
For you or for me.

Your hair (and its color) is lovely—
It almost sweeps the stars!
And it's done its job so far
By scheming with your smile and sweeping me off my feet.

If we were to part ways,
And all we had was the end of one last day,
I would sit in your car with you,
And watch you dance and bite your tongue
The way that you do.

I think you're absolutely beautiful.

I don't know if it's the way your eyes look,
Or the shape of your nose,
But I'm hooked;
Your brain intrigues me,
And your existence lightens my days;

Whatever it may be,
It touches a part of me in a certain way
That makes me think you're extraordinarily beautiful.

And I can't get over it.
I don't want to get over it.

I'm worried there's already a poem out there about you.
If there is, I pray that I went back in time and wrote it.

-For Miss Alma

You never wore lipstick,
But you always wore chapstick,
And it showed on every
Black coffee lid.

And I felt your chapstick with every kiss that was
Given and received.

But
I never saw you
Spit,
Or cry,
Or actually fall asleep.

I also never saw you cheat,
But it showed
In every text,
And I felt it in every utterance of
"I love you, too."

Cover a tattoo with another tattoo.
Cover a woman with another woman.

You look at her and smile,
But it feels empty;
It's felt this way for a while.
What is it?
Why do you feel so insincere?
Why do you feel like shit?
Whose fault was it in the first place?
Maybe it was no one's fault;
Maybe feelings sometimes lose their pace,
Or stop altogether:
Stop; lie down; and die.
Maybe love isn't meant to last forever.

She smiles back at you
And lets a sigh escape her nostrils;
She imagines her snot as morning dew.
Silly, stupid thoughts distract her
From the cold that you infect her with;
There was a time when she loved you, sure,
But there was also that time when you cheated,
And her emotions grew fatigued,
And her heart and soul became depleted;
She lacked the proper emotional nutrients from you,
So her feelings atrophied:
Withered and died (perhaps they were bound to).

Maybe love isn't meant to last forever,
And, when it does, it's and anomaly;
A force greater than time, gravity, or weather.

You place your hand in the forefront of your hair. You let the silky strands fill the spaces between your fingers, and then you begin to comb. Halfway across your scalp you worry that this may tamper with today's volume, but it doesn't worry you more than being bit by a puppy, so you continue. As your hand leaves the rested comfort of you head, it begins a controlled glide down the free of your hair, and you think of a prince—perhaps a tiny prince—sliding down your hair in much the same way a normal-sized prince would slide down Rapunzel's hair. But your thoughts are brought to a halt as your middle finger stumbles upon a knot. "I think not," you giggle, and force your finger through the barricade. You know you just damaged your hair, but no more than how blades of grass damage skin, so you continue to the end of your strands with a smile on your face.

A summer breeze
Not a cool breeze
Because it's summer
A rather warm breeze
But cool in comparison
To the bright heat of the sun
But it's still not cool
Deceitful

It's similar to how
An abusive relationship is
The abuser isn't abusing for a moment
And it feels nice
Like a summer breeze
But the abuser isn't being nice
The abuser just isn't abusing
Deceitful

Words hang from my mouth
Like when my brother would dangle spit over me
When we were young.

I hold onto my breath with the words;
Do I reel them back in like my brother did,
Or let them fall into your ears?

What if they fall too softly?
Or I stress the wrong word?
Or I stumble on the structure and fall?

Everyone stumbles from time to time,
But I feel as though I'd be the one to fall;
Would you be there to catch me?

All this scares me;
My friends say I think too much;
I think I think too much about you.

What would a man's man do?
What would my father do?
I don't think I could hear him through all the dirt.

I've always thought with my head and my heart,
But my sister says I should think with my other head;
My heart thinks that's bullshit.

Maybe I'll shut off all bodily processes
And become a robot;
That way I could forget the weight that words carry.

Or maybe I'll shout my words at you—
Full of emotion, passion, and spit;
Wait; what if I rupture your eardrums?

Stop; stop; stop; I need to stop:
I'm thinking too much again—
Intuition needs to take over my life.

An opportunity is being wasted
By my excessive thinking;
An opportunity to mix lives.

It'd be fantastic to share my life with you,
But what if you decline the offer?
But what if you don't?

I've come to conclude that it's better to put yourself out there
And get struck by lightning
Than to stay inside and die of lethargy.

So I'll let my words fall on you—
Like the time my brother went too far:
Because, in the end, I found myself laughing.

   -A Mouthful of Spit and Words

I wish the world were actually flat
    (So I could worry about falling off)

I wish I had a best friend named Matt
    (So we could watch our favorite wizard Gandalf)

I wish I didn't like non-sequiturs
    (Because they're overrated)

I wish I didn't want her
    (But I can't say that I hate it)

The light shoos away the night
Like a homeless dog,
Or when Adam and Eve were cast out by God;
Or like how depression overcomes life,
Which is opposite of light overcoming darkness—
Isn't it?

The forces wage war,
And lives are bent, broken, and torn;
Some hearts come out with a beat;
Other hearts lose themselves in the dark.
They listen for the thumps of others—
Dammit do they hark—
But they hear only their own blood flow,
And so the darkness grows:
Bigger, heavier, crushing.
The hearts become arrhythmic;
It all seems destroyed.
The darkness has taken over
And the beats cease.

A pothole in the road, in the eyes of drivers, has no business being there. But the pothole, in all reality, doesn't have business at all. That is because potholes aren't *anything*; they're just the absence of asphalt (much like the cliché that darkness is the absence of light). A pothole is the result of life inflicting itself upon a strip of road, which *is* a thing. Potholes are filled with rock and tar, but it's never the same—everyone can see the scar and the road itself can feel it. The road never asked to be laid, nor did it ask to be pounded on by metal and the heat from the sun. Perhaps the road longs to form potholes: the less of it there is, the less the road suffers.

Many potholes have formed throughout my life, but love and time have filled most of them—although you can still see the scars.

Nothing interests me more
Than what others find to be a bore;
Well, actually, that's a little untrue:
In general, I want what others do not.
Maybe that's why I want you:
Not that you're undesirable to others;
That's not true.
But maybe it's the fact that you don't want you.

I don't know where I'm going with this.
Love trumping depression is a myth,
A fairytale of sorts,
And I'm not this magical and dashing prince
Who has the power to sweep you off your feet,
Because you're not on your feet—are you?
You're curled on the floor, or your bed,
Crippled by sadness,
Like a semi caused this,
Or something large.
You're not on your feet,
At least not mentally.

I love the thought of love:
I will write endlessly about it,
And dream excessively about it;
But I tremble
When I find myself
On its front porch.

About the Author

Garrett Willis's new collection of short stories was inspired by the heartache he has experienced in his own life.

Willis is an English teacher hailing from Bakersfield, California. He received his bachelor's degree in English with a minor in theater.

Willis's Twitter: @Gwilballer
Cover Art by Anthony Chable (Instagram: @anthonychable)

Made in the USA
San Bernardino, CA
17 December 2017